## Good-bye Vacation, Hello Work...

Chris turned on the TV and plopped down in the oversized orange chair in front of it. A game show was on, but she didn't pay any attention to it. She was too busy thinking about the Palm Pavilion Hotel and wishing she'd never gotten up that morning.

How had she let Liza and Sam talk her into such a crazy idea?

Now her summer of loafing — the summer she had been looking forward to all year — was completely shot. She hadn't really expected that they'd get the baby-sitting jobs. But they had. And now she was stuck!

**Look for these other books in the
SITTING PRETTY series:**

# Chapter One

Christine Brown stretched out on her low platform bed and cracked back the spine of the fat paperback she held in her hands. "Alone at last," she whispered into the pages, then giggled softly at the silliness of talking to a book. But this wasn't just any plain old book. This was *The Big Book of TV Trivia*.

She had discovered it in the discount bin of Myer's Supermarket two days ago and hadn't had a chance

heard her mother say around the house. Chris thought that if she around here all going to st loaf ned to Chris that all the last-minute study- g she had done in order to avoid summer school had more than earned her the right to some good, solid loafing. After all, this was her last summer

1

before she started high school. She had to rest up for the challenging year ahead.

If only her busy-bee mother could understand that! Thankfully, summer school had finally started for those poor unfortunates who hadn't made the grade, and Chris's mother, who was a teacher, had to go back to work — leaving Chris alone with her trivia book.

She opened the book to the chapter titled "The Best of *The Brady Bunch*," and quickly scanned the facts. "I knew that," she mumbled as she read the already-familiar information. "I knew that, too."

She tossed back her chin-length strawberry-blond hair and sighed. She had so many books on trivia that it was hard to dig up new information, but when she did uncover a new tidbit, it was like finding hidden treasure.

She flipped to the next chapter, "All About *The Odd Couple*," and her face brightened. "Felix Unger's favorite opera was *Tosca* by Verdi," she read. "I didn't know that," she mumbled to herself. The book hadn't been a waste of money after

She was about to move on to
when she heard loud rapping on the meta
front screen door. Loud rapping on the metal
strained her back so she could edge of the bed, she
The house was on one level and her knocking.
just off the living room. If she twisted her head
the right angle, she could see who was standing out-

2

side. Summers in Bonita Beach, Florida, were so steamy hot that no one ever closed their inside doors unless they had air conditioning. Most people did, but the Browns had recently installed ceiling fans in an effort to cut down on their electric bills.

"Come on in, it's open!" she shouted when she spotted the two girls standing outside the door. The girls entered the house and headed for Chris's room.

"You shouldn't leave the door open like that," scolded Liza Velez as she stopped to lock the metal door from inside. "You don't know what kind of weirdoes could be lurking around out there."

"You mean like the two that just walked into my house?" Chris shot back playfully, not bothering to move from the bed.

"Very funny," said Samantha O'Neill, plopping down on the bed next to Chris. "I don't see how you can call *us* weird when you're the one lying around inside on a great day, reading your eight-zillionth trivia book." Her tone was serious, but her green eyes sparkled as she teased her friend. "It's not normal for a thirteen-year-old to know so much about shows that were made before she was even born."

"I'll be fourteen in three weeks," Chris reminded her.

"Oh, excuse me!" Sam laughed, shaking her head and setting her long ash-blond ponytail in motion. "That makes it even stranger."

"How can you stand to read another one of those

things?" Liza asked as she swung her lanky legs over Chris's desk chair so that she was sitting on it backwards. Some of her long brown hair was tied up into a ponytail at the top of her head; the rest fell loosely down to her elbows. She redid her hair elastic as she spoke. "I mean, just look at your bookshelf. It's nothing but trivia books."

"Hey, I like trivia, okay? I bet you can't name all the crew members on *Gilligan's Island*."

Liza rolled her eyes and began humming the theme song from the show, which aired in reruns every afternoon. "Okay, there was Gilligan, the Skipper, the professor, the millionaire . . . what was his name, oh, yeah, Thurston Howell."

"Thurston Howell *the Third*," Chris corrected her.

"Don't be so picky," Liza grumbled. "There was Mary Ann and Ginger — "

"All right, already!" Sam cried. "We didn't come over here to take a trivia test."

"Relax," said Chris, taking two red hoop earrings from her night table and threading them through her pierced ears. "What's the big deal?"

"The big deal is that we're all going to get jobs," said Sam, her face brightening into a smile.

"Over at the Palm Pavilion Hotel," Liza added.

"What!" Chris exclaimed in disbelief. She had lived in Bonita Beach all her life and she had never even been inside the huge, luxurious hotel. Though it sometimes seemed that half the people in Bonita Beach worked there, the Palm was so expensive that very few people in town ever stayed there, or even dined in one of their three fancy restaurants. "It's only June and you guys already have sunstroke," she said to her friends.

"No we don't," Sam assured her eagerly. "My sister, Greta, started working there as a waitress and she told me that they're starting a baby-sitting service for the guests and they're hiring baby sitters."

Liza stood and studied herself in the full-length mirror on the door of Chris's closet. She rolled up the sleeves of the short red-striped shirt she was wearing over a pair of white shorts. "Do you think they'll hire someone with braces?" she asked, grimacing.

"We'll never know if we don't try," said Sam. She bounced off the bed and headed for the door. "Hurry up and get ready, Chris. If we get this job then maybe I'll have a chance at a lifeguard job in a couple of years. Greta says they only hire kids to be lifeguards who have already worked there before. I would *love* to be a lifeguard at the Palm. That would mean I could spend every summer outside. It would be so great!"

"Hold on," Chris said. "I don't know anything about little kids! I've never baby-sat before. You guys at least have some experience."

Liza grunted. "I could handle anything after baby-sitting for my brothers, the twin terrors. If I don't get this job I'm going to be stuck sitting for them all summer — for free." Liza knelt to re-tie the red shoe-lace of her white sneaker. Her other sneaker was red with a white shoelace. "Plus it's at the *Palm Pavilion*, Chris. Think about it! There are always rich, famous people staying there. Maybe we'll get discovered."

"You think you're going to get discovered everywhere," Chris pointed out. "You put makeup on to go down to the supermarket, just in case a famous director or producer happens to be shopping at the same time."

"I just want to be prepared, that's all," Liza said with a shrug. "How else am I going to get into a movie? Bonita Beach isn't exactly Hollywood."

"Well, I don't care about being in a movie," Chris said, settling back on her bed.

"Don't you care about the money?" Sam coaxed. "Since I began baby-sitting for the Thompsons down the block, I've earned a lot. If we get these jobs I'll be able to buy that new ten-speed I want pretty soon."

"I don't know," said Chris, biting her nails. "My allowance covers everything I need."

"Oh, you're just being chicken," said Sam, throwing up her arms in frustration.

A mischievous gleam came into Liza's dark brown eyes. "I know what will get you to come with us. I heard that a certain someone is working at the Palm this summer . . . ."

"Who?" Chris asked, frowning.

"Someone with big blue eyes and blond hair that kind of flops into his eyes."

"No!" gasped Chris.

"Yes. None other than *the* Bruce Johnson, the boy

6

of your dreams," Liza replied.

"I didn't know Chris liked Bruce Johnson," Sam said.

"Like him!" cried Liza. "Her eyes start spinning in her head every time he walks by and she kind of starts breathing like this." Liza stuck out her tongue and began panting like a dog on a hot day.

"Cut it out," Chris said, trying not to smile as she tossed the trivia book at her friend. "Who wouldn't like Bruce Johnson? He's only totally gorgeous."

"Then this is your golden opportunity to spend a whole summer with him," Liza prodded.

"We-ell." Chris slowly got up off the bed. "You guys aren't going to leave me alone until I come with you, anyway."

Sam slapped her on the back. "That's what friends are for — to nudge you to death until you do what they want you to do."

Liza giggled. "I knew the bit about Bruce Johnson would get her."

Chris grabbed a peach sweat shirt and tied the arms of it around her neck. It was nearly ninety degrees, but she didn't like to go out wearing just a T-shirt and shorts. She was self-conscious about the extra ten pounds she needed to lose in order to look like all the pretty, thin teen-agers who seemed to abound in Bonita Beach. "Maybe we should go tomorrow," she said, hesitating in front of the mirror. "My chin is all broken out."

"And you think it's going to be cleared up by tomorrow?" Liza asked.

Sam pushed up her straight bangs. "Look at my forehead. I'm not letting a few zits stop *me*."

"Easy for you to say; you wear bangs," Chris protested.

Liza grabbed Chris by the sleeve of her T-shirt and pulled her out of her bedroom. "Quit stalling and come on."

The three girls left the house and rode their bikes down Vine Street. After ten minutes, they came to the center of town. It was really nothing more than a series of small, one-story shopping arcades, some restaurants and bars, a movie theater, a cluster of government buildings, and then more stores and restaurants.

Once they were on the other side of town, the sidewalks became patchy, turning into dirt paths in places, until finally they ended altogether. The small shops and buildings along the main road grew fewer and farther apart, until the girls were on a dirt road densely surrounded with lush palms on either side. The road's only purpose was to lead visitors to the hotel, which was tucked away out of sight. In other words, you had to know where it was in order to get there — and that was what celebrities liked most about the Palm Pavilion.

After ten minutes on the bumpy dirt road, Chris stopped pedaling her old three-speed and brushed the sweat from her brow with the back of her hand. "Oh, man, I can't take this," she called to her friends, who were several feet ahead of her.

Liza stopped and placed her feet on the ground. "It's not much farther!" she called back, but her chest was heaving from the effort of cycling, and wisps of brown hair were sticking to her face.

It took athletic Sam a few more minutes to realize her friends had stopped. "Come on," she yelled, putting her feet down and skidding to a stop.

Slowly but steadily Liza and Chris caught up with Sam. "If we get these jobs, the first thing I'm buying is a motorbike," Liza said between gasps for breath.

"You're not old enough to drive one," Chris pointed out.

"Tough," said Liza. "I'll lie about my age."

"Maybe Greta will drive us on days when she can get the car," Sam suggested. "I'm pretty sure the hotel is just around the next bend."

" 'Just!' " Chris quipped sarcastically. "The curve in the road is about a mile away! No job is worth dying for," she proclaimed.

"Chris, it's only about five hundred yards," Sam argued. "And once you get there, it's only another hundred yards or so, right toward the water. It *is* worth it — wait until you see the inside of the hotel! Greta says it's like something out of a movie."

"The Palm Pavilion is heavenly," Liza said with a sigh.

"Have you ever been there?" asked Chris.

"Once, right before my parents got divorced. They

hired a baby sitter for the twins and the three of us went to dinner there. It was supposed to be to celebrate my tenth birthday, but I think it was really some last-ditch effort to save their marriage." Liza looked wistful for a moment. "My memory is a little blurry, but I remember that the hotel was like being in a fantasy land . . . like . . . like . . . " She shrugged her shoulders. "Like heaven."

"Break time is over," said Sam crisply. She loved any kind of physical activity, and the long bike ride was no problem for her sturdy legs.

The girls resumed their journey up the dirt road, and five minutes later they reached the main gateway to the hotel.

"There it is!" Sam announced.

The three of them gazed at the huge, rose-colored hotel that lay less than a quarter of a mile away, at the end of a white gravel drive lined with palm trees.

Chris squinted. The white-shuttered windows seemed to glisten in the sunlight. She cocked her head and listened. She heard the low humming of insects, and the gentle rustle of the surrounding palms waving in the breeze that blew up from the sparkling blue ocean just behind the hotel.

It all seemed eerily quiet and very strange. Chris almost wanted to turn around and cycle home. The place was bigger and grander than she had imagined. She looked at her friends, and from their stunned expressions she could tell that they were equally awed.

"It's even more beautiful than I remembered," whispered Liza.

"Gosh," Sam murmured as they rode their bikes under a majestic archway. "I feel like I died and . . . "

"Went to heaven," Liza finished, nodding. The three friends looked at one another, unsure of whether or not to proceed.

"Hey, what are we waiting for?" Sam said with a nervous laugh. Not waiting for their answer, she jumped off her bike and ditched it in the bushes. "Let's go," she urged.

Liza looked at Chris and shrugged. "What have we got to lose?"

# Chapter Two

Chris stood in the doorway of the hotel and looked around the spacious, elegant lobby. In front of her was a large, rough slate wall with a waterfall cascading down its surface. Beyond it, down a level, was the main section of the blue- and pink-tiled lobby with its antique furniture. Dark wood chairs cushioned in shades of dusty green and blue were clustered together around low tables. Thick, round mahogany columns reached up to the cathedral-style ceiling. Real palm trees and rubber plants sat in huge brass pots, growing under the skylight in the middle of the ceiling.

An open balcony on the second level contained a lounge, where a piano player was already performing for the lunch crowd. Large golden cages filled with tropical birds hung from the ceiling around the lounge.

After the brightness and heat of outdoors, the

lobby seemed cool and very dark. "I wish the fans in our house worked this well," said Chris, looking up at the large, wooden fans that whirred silently overhead. With a small shiver, she untied the arms of the peach sweat shirt she'd draped over her shoulders and slipped it over her head.

Liza rolled her eyes. "This place is completely air-conditioned. Those fans are just for effect."

"I *thought* they were a little too good," Chris replied with an embarrassed laugh.

"Cute outfits," Sam commented, nodding her head in the direction of two girls heading across the lobby carrying trays of glasses upstairs to the lounge. Both waitresses wore identical staff uniforms: Palm Pavilion polo shirts, walking shorts and white leather sneakers.

"I don't know," muttered Chris, wondering how she'd look in the trim cotton shirt and silently vowing not to eat another chocolate chip cookie as long as she lived — or at least until she lost ten pounds.

"The people who work here sure get the good-grooming award," Liza commented, noting the neat haircuts and crisp, ironed look of all the staff members. She smoothed down the front of her slightly wrinkled shorts. "Maybe we should have dressed fancier."

"Too late now. Come on," said Sam, heading down into the lobby. They headed for the main registration desk, where smiling men and women were checking guests in and out.

They asked about the baby-sitting positions and were directed to a door at the end of the registration counter. "Mr. Parker is the manager," a petite Oriental woman informed them. "You have to talk to him." They approached the door, which was open a crack. Sam raised her hand to knock, but stopped when they heard the sound of a man's voice bellowing from inside.

"What do you mean, the oysters are all bad!" he screeched. "Well, what moron left them lying out on the dock? Are they *all* bad? . . . Well, find out! . . . I don't care if it will make you sick. This is making *me* sick!" They heard the sound of a phone slamming down.

"It doesn't sound like Mr. Parker is in a very good mood," whispered Chris in a worried voice. "Maybe we should come back later."

At that moment the door flew wide open and they were staring up at a tall, pencil-thin man with piercing blue eyes, a long, sharp nose and thin lips. He wore a blue cotton button-down shirt and navy blue shorts that were belted high on his waist. The sparse hair on the top of his head was combed across his bald spot to make it look as if he had more hair than he actually did. He almost walked right into the three girls.

"First the caviar order is lost, then the oysters go bad and now I'm invaded by Munchkins," he complained to the air. "What is it, ladies?"

The girls looked at one another nervously.

"Ummmm," Sam began. "My sister Greta told me . . . do you know her? She works here."

"Young lady, there are over two hundred employees at this hotel. I could not possibly know each one by name. Please get to the point. I have a disaster to attend to in the kitchen."

"Okay," Sam said, speaking rapidly. "She said you were hiring baby sitters, so we're here to apply for the job."

Mr. Parker studied them skeptically. "How old are you girls? Twelve? Thirteen?"

"Fourteen," Liza said, sounding hurt. She had just turned fourteen, and she thought she looked every inch of it.

Mr. Parker shook his head. "No, I'm sorry. You're simply too young. Now I must go." He walked off briskly, but the girls trailed him.

"I have lots of experience," Sam said, jogging along beside him. "I've been baby-sitting for over two years now."

"Me, too," Liza said, hurrying next to Sam. She looked back at Chris, who was lagging behind them. "And Christine has ten little brothers and sisters, so she's almost a professional," Liza added.

Chris's eyes went wide at the lie, but she kept quiet.

Mr. Parker stopped and faced them. "I'm sure you girls would do fine if everything went well, but I need baby sitters who can cope with any crisis that should arise."

15

"We could," Sam insisted. "I took a Red Cross first aid course after school last year."

"I'm sure you're a regular little lifesaver," said Mr. Parker impatiently, "but my answer is still no. Now, if you'll excuse me."

At that moment they heard a woman scream in the upstairs lounge. She screamed again, and several other people started shouting.

Mr. Parker sighed loudly. "What now?" he muttered as he hurried toward the stairs to the lounge.

The girls followed him to the center of the lobby, where he stopped and looked up — just as everyone else in the lobby seemed to be doing. What they saw was a very large green-and-yellow parrot with a red head swooping low over the tables in the lounge, knocking over drinks and occasionally stopping to peck at the salted peanuts before moving on.

A pretty girl with a blond ponytail bouncing behind her came racing down the stairs. "Mr. Parker, I'm so sorry," she wailed. "A customer asked to see Pitpat up close, so I thought I'd take him out of his cage for just a second."

Mr. Parker's face turned a bright shade of red. "You know that is against the rules," he scolded.

The girl looked ashamed. "I'm sorry. The man offered me a twenty-dollar tip and I didn't think it would hurt," she admitted in a small voice. "I thought his wings were clipped."

"So did I," said Mr. Parker, looking up at the swooping bird.

A middle-aged woman with a head of silver hair swept up into a high, elaborate hairdo came stumbling down the stairs holding her straw clutch bag over her head. "Mercy! That bird dove for my hair!" she cried in a voice thick with a Texas accent. "He actually touched it. He must have thought it was a nest or something!"

Chris, Sam and Liza bit their lips, trying not to laugh. "It looks like a nest to me," Chris whispered, letting a small giggle escape her lips.

Before Mr. Parker could apologize to the woman, there was another roar of voices from above. Pitpat the parrot had soared out of the lounge and was now swooping quickly through the lobby in a blur of yellow, green and red feathers.

"Wow, his wings are really huge when he spreads them out," Sam observed, craning her neck back to see the bird. "He does look a little scary." A shrill squawk from the bird made her jump. "He's loud, too."

By now the lobby was in chaos. Guests ran for cover as the bird dove low to help himself to their plates of nuts. Tall tropical drinks toppled as Pitpat tried unsuccessfully to perch on their rims and take a sip. Three bus boys tried to catch the parrot when he settled briefly on the branch of a low palm, but they succeeded only in knocking over the large potted plant and scaring Pitpat all the way up to the top branch of a tall palm tree just beside the balcony.

Once he was on top of the tree, Pitpat showed off

his talent for speaking by showering the guests with off-color phrases and insults. People hurried their children out of earshot. Two blue-haired ladies huffed indignantly at Mr. Parker as they hobbled past him.

"I knew I should have stayed in bed today," Mr. Parker muttered to himself. He turned to a group of waiters and waitresses who had gathered nearby. "Where did Pitpat learn to talk like that?" he demanded.

The group looked at Mr. Parker and seemed to shrug all at once. "Chef Alleyne likes to feed him in the kitchen sometimes," suggested a tan young man with a blond crewcut. "Things can get a little nasty in there when we get real busy. Maybe that's where he picked up these . . . uh . . . phrases."

"Shut up or I cut you into little pieces!" screamed the bird. "Little pieces! *Awk!* Little pieces!"

Mr. Parker shook his head. "Yes, that *does* sound like Chef Alleyne's influence." He looked as if he were about to be very ill. "A bird in the kitchen," he whimpered. "A bird in the kitchen. The board of health would have us shut down in a second if they got wind of this. We have to get that bird immediately."

"My father had a parrot for years," said Liza. "Sometimes if you sort of sang his name in a sweet voice he'd come to you."

"I saw a *Gilligan's Island* episode the other day, where a parrot flew away with Mrs. Howell's diamonds," said Chris. "Gilligan got him down from a tree by luring him with marshmallows. The Skipper

18

was very mad because they were his last bag."

Sam reached into her pocket and pulled out a half-eaten bag of sunflower seeds. "Do you think he'd like these?" she asked, casting a questioning glance in Mr. Parker's direction.

"Try anything, I don't care. I'm desperate," he answered.

The girls ran up the grand staircase and into the now-empty Parrot Lounge. Sam poured out a handful of seeds. Bracing herself against the railing, she leaned out over the wooden rail of the balcony as far as she could.

"Careful," warned Chris, holding onto the back of her shirt. "Don't fall."

"Here Pitpat, Pitpat, Pitpat," Liza sang in the sweet, gentle voice that had always worked with her father's parrot. She clucked softly with her tongue and then continued, "Here Pitpat, Pitpat, Pitpat."

Pitpat was on the branch of a palm about two feet from Sam's outstretched hands. He looked in the direction of Liza's voice and blinked his beady black eyes. "Idiots!" he screeched, cocking his head. "All waiters are idiots!"

"I'm glad we're not waiters." Sam laughed. "Hey, what do I do if I get him?"

"Give him to me," Liza whispered. "I know how to hold him."

Liza continued to call to the parrot while Sam jiggled the seeds in her hand. Chris wrapped her arms around Sam's waist and held tight, fearful that

Sam would bend too far out over the railing and end her days in a heap on top of Mr. Parker below.

Suddenly, Pitpat flapped his colorful wings and hopped onto Sam's hand. *"Oowww!"* she cried. "His nails are sharp. And he's heavy."

"Shhhh!" Liza hushed her. "You'll scare him. Pull him in nice and easy and I'll grab him."

"I've got you, Sam." Chris grunted as she felt her friend's weight shift forward with the effort of pulling in the large bird.

As soon as the bird was a few inches from the rail, Liza grabbed his two legs with her left hand and tucked him under her right arm. "Give him more seeds," she urged Sam as the powerful bird squirmed.

Almost immediately, a dark-haired, handsome bartender and Mr. Parker appeared at her side carrying a large cage. Liza got up close to the door and carefully shoved the parrot inside. "You know, I don't really blame this bird," she said to Mr. Parker. "It's mean to keep him cooped up in a cage."

Mr. Parker raised an eyebrow at her comment, but the bartender smiled. "We keep all the birds in a large aviary on the grounds," he told her, "and we rotate the ones who appear in the lounge every few days."

"Satisfied?" Mr. Parker asked.

"Yes, I guess that's okay," Liza conceded. "But I still think you could keep them on perches instead of cages. You could tie one leg so they can't go too far."

"I believe that's against sanitary codes, but I will

take it under consideration," said Mr. Parker.

"Can I give these kids sodas and some chips on the house, Mr. Parker?" asked the bartender. "I'd say they did a great job."

"I suppose we do owe them something for their efforts," agreed Mr. Parker.

"You know what we'd rather have?" Sam asked boldly. "Jobs."

"I told you girls — " Mr. Parker began to protest.

"I think we've proved that we can handle an emergency," Sam pressed.

At that, the bartender chuckled. "You sure thought faster than anyone else around here," he said, casting a meaningful glance at Mr. Parker.

Mr. Parker looked as though he felt trapped. "Oh — oh — " he sputtered. "All right. But you are on trial. If you slip up, come in late, *anything* — you're out. Go downstairs and get your polo shirts from Mrs. Chan at the registration desk. All staff baby sitters must wear neat shorts that match their shirts — and I expect to see you all in new white sneakers on your first day of work," he said, staring down at Liza's red and white ones.

"Sure thing, Mr. Parker," agreed Liza, fidgeting nervously.

Sam reached to shake his hand, but Mr. Parker was already off down the stairs. "Thanks," she called after him.

Still smiling to himself, the bartender took Pitpat back to his spot over the bar.

21

"We did it! We did it!" Liza squealed. "We're working at the Palm Pavilion! Way to go!"

Sam's eyes sparkled, but Chris was worried. "I don't know," she said. "I sure hope every day isn't this exciting."

# Chapter Three

Chris let the screen door slam as she entered her living room. "Chris! Please don't slam that door. I've asked you a thousand times," her mother called from the kitchen.

"Sorry," Chris mumbled. She turned on the TV and plopped down in the oversized orange chair in front of it. A game show was on, but Chris didn't pay any attention to it. She was too busy thinking about the Palm Pavilion and wishing she had never gotten up that morning.

How had she let Liza and Sam talk her into such a crazy idea?

Now her summer of loafing — the summer she had looked forward to all through the eighth grade — was completely shot. And she hadn't seen any sign of Bruce Johnson at the hotel, either! She hadn't really expected that they'd get the baby-sitting jobs. But they had, and now she was stuck.

She squirmed in the chair, trying to get comfortable. It seemed to her that the overhead fan was blowing hot air down, right on top of her head. "Some friends," she mumbled, pressing the TV remote and scanning the channels for something interesting to watch. She decided on a police show, but it turned out to be an episode she'd already seen.

Chris was trying to be angry at Liza and Sam, but she couldn't be, not really. In her heart she had to admit that the real reason she didn't want the job was because she was just plain scared. That cranky old Mr. Parker would be watching them like a hawk. And the hotel was so big and fancy. She'd never seen anything like it before. What if she made mistakes? Embarrassed herself? Failed miserably?

It wouldn't be the first time. When Chris's mother had enrolled her in Mrs. Thomas's School of Dance, Chris hadn't been able to stay in step with the other girls, no matter how hard she tried. Mrs. Thomas herself had requested that Chris leave the school.

Then there were the intramural sports that her mother was always insisting she try out for. Chris swore that she was allergic to balls of any kind. They seemed to swerve the other way whenever she got near one. She couldn't hit a baseball, dribble a basketball, kick a soccer ball or connect with a tennis ball. Her sports experience consisted of chasing after various balls as they rolled away from her.

Chris had come to the conclusion long ago that it was better not to attempt to do new things. That way you couldn't flop at them. Now, here was a great big new thing — just ready and waiting for her to foul up.

She clicked off the TV and went over to the screen door. She stood gazing absently out at the quiet street. This whole job situation presented a real problem. Normally, she would have found some way to get out of it — pretend to be sick, make up an excuse. But if she did that now, she'd have no one to hang out with all summer. Liza and Sam would be busy working at the hotel. Even Chris could stand to read only so many trivia books. Without her two best friends, it would be a long, boring summer.

"What are you looking at?" asked Chris's mother, coming up behind her.

Chris turned and looked directly into her mother's dark brown eyes. Five feet tall, Chris was only two inches shorter than her mother. She prayed that she'd take after her father's taller side of the family and grow to be at least five-foot-six. In fact, she hoped she wouldn't look a thing like her mother — with her short gray hair, plain, sporty way of dressing and her thick glasses — when she got older.

She *knew* she wouldn't actually *be* like her mother, since they weren't at all alike now. Mrs. Brown was a tiny dynamo; a bundle of energy who never seemed to tire. Chris, on the other hand, liked to take life at a more leisurely pace.

"I'm not looking at anything," Chris answered with a shrug. "I was just thinking about stuff."

"What stuff?" her mother asked, wiping her glasses on the checked apron she wore over her tan cotton pants.

"Just stuff," Chris said, evading the question.

Mrs. Brown sighed. "Christine, would you like to talk about this 'stuff?'"

"No, thanks," Chris answered. Her mother would think it was great that she'd gotten a job. She'd be thrilled. Overwhelmed. Ecstatic. Chris couldn't deal with that. It would just make it all the more difficult for Chris when everything fell apart.

"I hear you girls went to the Palm Pavilion to get jobs today," said her mother.

Chris threw up her arms. "You can't keep anything a secret in this town!" she shouted.

Her mother looked surprised. "I didn't know it was a secret. I ran into Mrs. Velez at the supermarket. She said Liza's very excited. I think that's wonderful, Chris."

"Well, I don't think it's going to last very long," Chris said sullenly.

"Why not?"

"There's this guy named Mr. Parker who runs the place and he hates us already. He just got forced into hiring us because we caught his parrot."

"What?" her mother asked. She'd taken off her apron and was dusting the furniture with it as they spoke.

"It's a long story," said Chris.

"Well, I think you'll make a terrific baby sitter,"

26

said her mother.

"Mom!" Chris groaned. "You thought I'd make a great dancer, a wonderful softball player, a terrific musician, a super water-skier. And can I do any of those things? No!"

"The important thing is you tried. I still say you'd be good at all those things if you stuck with them. You give up too easily," Mrs. Brown stated. "You know, you don't get anywhere in life by being a quitter."

"I'm not a quitter. I'm a klutz!" Chris argued.

Her mother stopped dusting. "Christine, I don't want to hear that kind of talk. You can do anything you set your mind to."

"Maybe *you* can, but I can't."

"Christine — "

"I don't want to talk about this anymore," Chris said, cutting off her mother. What was the point? She knew what her mother was going to say. She'd heard it a thousand times. She'd say it was all in Chris's head, that she had a defeatist attitude. Then she'd say she didn't know where Chris had picked up such a negative outlook. It certainly wasn't from her or from Chris's father. Chris had to agree there. Her mother and her father, who was the manager of a restaurant, were go-getters.

"I'm bound to get fired from this job and then you'll bug me about it," Chris snapped.

"When have I ever bugged you about things you tried that didn't turn out?" protested her mother.

"Okay," Chris admitted, "but you bug me in your head."

"What?" asked her mother, wearing an expression of amused puzzlement.

"Oh, you know what I mean," said Chris, annoyed. "You don't say anything, but I know what you're thinking. 'Chris just didn't try hard enough. Again!' And you say it's okay with this saintly face on."

"Show me my saintly face," her mother teased.

"Don't make fun of me!" Chris shouted, angry tears filling her eyes. "You don't understand! You don't understand how it feels to always be a flop!"

Chris turned and fled into her room. She threw herself down on her bed and sobbed. Why was everyone always pushing her to try new things? She was perfectly content to stay with the things she knew — going to school, hanging out with her friends, reading and learning about trivia. Wasn't that enough?

She let the tears stream down her cheeks until her pillowcase was wet. Then she sat up and rubbed her eyes with the palms of her hands. Realistically, things weren't any brighter, but she always felt better after a good cry.

In a few minutes there was a knock on her door. "Come in," she said with a sniffle.

Her mother came in and sat down on her bed. She pulled a small pack of tissues from her pants pocket and handed one to Chris. Chris smiled. Leave it to her super-organized mother to have a supply of clean tissues right at hand.

"Chris," her mother began in a calm voice. "The only reason I push you to try new things is because I want you to get the most out of life — not because I want to torment you."

"I know," said Chris. "I'm just not good at anything."

"That's not true," Mrs. Brown argued. "You're bright, you're funny and you have a very good heart."

"Thanks," said Chris, enjoying her mother's compliments. "But that still doesn't make me good at anything."

"Maybe you simply haven't found your thing yet — as we used to say back in the sixties. When you find something you really like, then you'll be good at it."

"You think so?" Chris asked.

"I'm sure of it," said her mother, rising from her bed. "You like trivia, for instance, and you're a whiz at it."

"That's true," Chris said with a smile. "Maybe you're right."

"I'm sure I am." Her mother winked and turned to go. "Supper's in half an hour."

"Okay. And you don't really have a saintly face, Mom," said Chris.

Her mother laughed. "Thanks. . . I think."

When her mother left, Chris opened the bottom drawer of her dresser and pulled out two cellophane packages. One contained a white polo shirt and the other a pink polo shirt; both bore the Palm Pavilion Hotel insignia. Mrs. Chan at the front desk had given them to the girls when they had gone to the desk to file their employment applications with her. She had told them that they could wear the shirts with whatever they wanted, shorts or miniskirts, as long as they looked neat and coordinated. Tomorrow, Tuesday, Chris would have to buy a pair of new white sneakers, and Wednesday would be her first day as a staff baby sitter for the hotel.

She opened up the packages and laid them out on the bed. The shirts looked so neat and crisp. She held the pink one up to her chest and stood in front of her mirror. She tried to imagine her first customer standing before her. "Hi," she said, grinning into the mirror. "My name is Chris and I'm your baby satter . . . I mean saby bitter . . . "

She sighed and leaned her forehead against the mirror — and prayed that Wednesday would never come.

# *Chapter Four*

The girls chained their bikes to the rack off to the side of the hotel. It was eight-thirty Wednesday morning and they were reporting for their first day of work.

"Oh, no! I got dirt on these shorts already," moaned Liza, frantically rubbing a smudge from her freshly washed blue shorts.

"Maybe we'd better go back," Chris suggested anxiously. "Liza's dirty and I'm all sweaty. We wouldn't want to make a bad impression on our first day."

"How could you be sweaty at eight-thirty in the morning?" Sam asked. "It's not even hot yet."

"It's a long bike ride and it makes me sweaty," Chris complained. "I doubt anyone wants a sweaty baby sitter."

"Come on, you guys," Sam urged. "I'm nervous, too. But we just have to go in there and do it."

Liza frowned at Sam. "Do you jocks always have a

31

pep talk ready for every occasion?"

Sam stuck out her tongue. "You don't have to get mean just because you're scared."

"Okay, okay, you're right," Liza admitted. "Let's go."

They walked past the front toward the side service entrance of the hotel, as Mrs. Chan had instructed them to do. The hotel grounds seemed so different this early in the day. On Monday, the front entrance had been congested with people and cabs. Now the only people in sight were two gardeners. One clipped the hedges and the other rode a power mower across the lawn, filling the air with the warm, sweet smell of newly mowed grass.

"The ocean sounds so loud," said Sam, listening to the rumble of the nearby surf. "I wonder why."

"It just sounds loud because it's so much more quiet now than during the day," said Chris. She stopped for a moment and concentrated on the sound of the waves. It always had a calming effect on her.

As they approached the service entrance near the kitchen, they heard the sound of clanking dishes. Two trucks were parked in the side drive. One truck said ALL STATE SEAFOOD on the side and the other had the words BART'S BEVERAGES printed on its door. In front of them was a blue van, from which a man in blue overalls was delivering bags of bread.

"Isn't it exciting, being behind the scenes like this?" said Liza. "I feel like I'm in the opening scene of a movie about a girl who starts out as a lowly baby

32

sitter, but is discovered by a famous movie director and becomes a great star."

"That's you, of course," said Sam.

"Of course," Liza said. "Isn't that obvious? The movie will end with me pulling up in a red Porsche, draped in furs, coming back to the same hotel where I got my first job — but this time, as a star!"

"You have some imagination," Chris laughed.

Liza put her hand over her heart dramatically. "It's not imagination. It's destiny. It's what I am fated to — "

"Excuse me, coming through," a gruff voice interrupted. Liza looked up and saw a man in gray coveralls heading toward her, pushing a dolly filled with soda cans. She had to jump out of the path to avoid him.

"Hey, watch it!" she shouted after him. "You almost creamed a star."

"Sorry, kid," the man called back over his shoulder.

"Hmmmph," Liza snorted. "Some people don't recognize greatness when they see it."

Sam shook her head and grabbed Liza by the wrist. "Come on, star. We have to go meet a few more people who probably won't recognize your greatness, either."

"Maybe they won't recognize it right away," said Liza as the three of them approached the wood-framed screen door of the service entrance. They hung back, not certain they were supposed to go into what was obviously the kitchen. Two girls wearing staff shirts came up behind them and walked through the door. They looked like twins with their long, straight blond hair.

"This must be the place," said Sam. She pulled open the door and the girls stepped in. Immediately they were surrounded by the sounds of people talking and the smell of food cooking.

"Hey, look! Look!" Sam cried excitedly. "There are our names." She ran over to a time clock mounted on the wall a few feet away from the door. Below the clock was a metal holder, full of manila cards with names printed on them. On the last three cards were the names Christine Brown, Samantha O'Neill and Elizabeth Velez. "Oh, yuck, I hope everyone doesn't start calling me Samantha," Sam grunted, lifting her card from its slot.

"Try Elizabeth," added Liza, wrinkling up her nose.

"What are we supposed to do with these?" asked Chris.

Liza and Sam looked at her and shrugged. At that moment, the bartender they'd met the other day came in, looking like he'd just rolled out of bed. He pulled a card marked Raoul Smith out of a slot and punched it into another slot just below the clock. He stood back and squinted at the blue mark the clock had printed on his card. "Eight-thirty-five," he mumbled sourly, reading the time off his card. "What sane person is at work at eight-thirty-five in the morning?"

"You're here," Liza observed cheerfully.

"I have to stock the bar this morning," he said,

looking at her with bleary eyes. He bent down and stuck his face right into Liza's. "And who said I was sane?" he yelled.

Liza jumped back, a surprised look on her face. "Boy, remind me to steer clear of him in the mornings," she huffed as Raoul stalked off.

"I guess he's not what you'd call a morning person," agreed Sam.

The girls followed Raoul's example and punched their cards into the slot below the clock. "Isn't this cool?" gushed Liza. "We're actually punching a time clock."

"My father says he hates punching the time clock," said Chris.

"Well, I've never punched one before and I think it's neat," Liza insisted.

The girls made their way through the noisy, bustling kitchen. Everyone was so wrapped up in their own business that no one gave them a second glance. Suddenly a loud thud startled the girls. They looked and saw that a very fat man dressed in white had just thrown a large carving knife down onto the wooden counter top.

"Where are my sliced mushrooms?" he bellowed angrily, shaking his head of wild red hair.

At that moment, Mr. Parker came hurrying into the kitchen. "Chef Alleyne, I must have a word with you — now," he declared.

"No one talks to Chef Alleyne until Chef Alleyne finds out where his mushrooms are!" the man shouted, his face turning beet red.

"Let's get out of here," whispered Chris, feeling her hands start to tremble.

They headed out the kitchen door and emerged into one of the hotel's four-star restaurants. The chairs were cushioned in blue velvet and stood on a thick green carpet. Huge watercolors of ocean scenes hung on the walls. The only sound was the low hum of the vacuum cleaner as a maid ran it across the rug. Compared to the hubbub in the kitchen, the restaurant was a sea of calm.

"There's Mrs. Chan," said Sam, pointing to the woman sitting at a table in the far corner of the restaurant.

Mrs. Chan looked up and smiled when she saw them approaching. "I'm just making up the assignment list for today," she said pleasantly. "Mr. Parker usually does this, but sometimes I take over when he has emergencies to deal with."

"Seems like he has lots of those," observed Sam.

"Mmmmm, yes indeed," said Mrs. Chan. Her expression was serious but there was a hint of laughter in her eyes as she spoke. "Did Mr. Parker mention to you that if we don't have enough baby-sitting assignments on a particular day, you'll be asked to do other odd jobs around the hotel?"

"No problem," Sam said quickly, before Mrs. Chan could notice the horrified look on Chris's face. "We're here to work."

"That's what I like to hear," said Mrs. Chan. "I

haven't finished the assignment sheet yet. Why don't you go wait by the front desk? I'll have it posted in fifteen minutes."

Sam, Chris and Liza went out into the quiet lobby. A few guests were already up and dressed in their bathing suits, heading outside to either the ocean or one of the three pools.

Suddenly Chris grabbed Liza and Sam by their arms. "It's him," she whispered frantically. "Over there."

Chris felt as if her knees would buckle under her. Bruce Johnson was standing beside one of the palm trees in the lobby. Somehow, he had gotten more handsome in the two short weeks since she'd last seen him. "Doesn't he look taller to you?" she asked Liza and Sam.

"No," Liza answered flatly.

"Yes, yes, he's definitely taller," Chris mumbled, trying not to panic. Bruce was a year ahead of them in school, but she had never even spoken to him. She had simply worshipped him from afar for years. Then, last year he'd gone off to Bonita Beach High and she hadn't seen him at all — except for glimpses of him at the beach or on the street. Now she might have to actually *talk* to him! "What am I going to do? He's really here."

"What's the problem?" asked Sam. "You were in the same school with him for years."

"That was different. There were always lots of people around."

"This isn't exactly a desert island, Chris," Liza reminded her. "There are a lot of people here now, too."

"No, this is different, you don't understand," Chris insisted. She looked over at Bruce again and saw that he was talking to someone who was hidden by the tree's large leaves.

"This is your chance," urged Sam. "Go over and talk to him."

"I couldn't," said Chris. "He doesn't even know who I am."

"He might recognize you from school. Ask him something about the hotel. It's a natural excuse to talk to him. Ask him when they put up the assignment sheet," suggested Liza.

"Mrs. Chan said it would be up in fifteen minutes," said Chris.

Sam gave Chris a gentle shove. "Don't be so dense. *We* know when the sheet is going up, but *he* doesn't know we know. So ask him."

Chris grinned despite her nervousness. "I get it. You know, Sam, you're not as innocent as you look. I like that."

"Just go talk to him!" Liza practically yelled.

"Okay, okay. Why not?" Chris breathed deeply and headed over toward Bruce. *Excuse me, you wouldn't happen to know when the assignment sheet goes up, would you?* she rehearsed in her head. *No, I need something more interesting. . . . "Mr. Parker will kill me if I don't find that assignment sheet. Do you know where I can find it?" . . . No, too flaky-sounding. . . .*

*"Hey, what time does that stupid sheet go up around here, anyway?"*

As Chris approached him, she pretended to be engrossed in looking up at the Parrot Lounge above her. She figured that way it wouldn't look as if she were deliberately heading over to talk to him. It would be more casual if it seemed that she just *happened* to ask the first person she saw . . . which, of course, would just happen to be him.

Chris's heart began to pound as she neared Bruce. Though she wasn't looking directly at him, she could sense his good-looking presence.

She stopped a few feet away from him. "Say, do you know when the assignment sheet goes up?" she said.

Bruce didn't seem to realize that she was talking to him. He didn't even look at her.

Panicked, Chris glanced over at Sam and Liza. They were standing together near the registration desk. With small fluttering hand motions, they signaled her to try again.

"Excuse me," Chris repeated in a voice that sounded just a bit too loud to her. Bruce turned around, but he didn't seem to recognize her. "Ummm, excuse me," Chris repeated. "Could you tell me when the. . . ummm. . . what do you call that thing again?"

"I don't know," he said. "What thing?"

"You know what I mean, the ummm, ummm . . . paper with the jobs on it." Chris wanted to die. Why had her mind picked this minute to go blank?

"Do you mean the assignment sheet?" asked Bruce,

looking at her as if she were a lunatic.

"That's it!" she cried with a nervous giggle. "The assignment sheet!"

"It should be out any minute now," he said.

*Now what?* Chris wondered. She stood there wishing she was Captain Kirk from *Star Trek* and that someone would beam her up out of this embarrassing situation. But no one did. Bruce stood there and looked at her. She either had to say something or leave. Nothing came to her.

"Hello, Christine!" a familiar voice called out.

Chris looked around, and her heart sank. It was Jannette Sansibar, the prettiest girl in the whole eighth grade. And — as far as Chris, Liza and Sam were concerned — the most annoying. Jannette was the ultimate goody-goody, always buttering up their teachers. She'd been in their class since third grade and they were constantly being told to be "more like Jannette."

Jannette also had a well-deserved reputation as the school's number-one tattletale. Once, in fourth grade, Liza had told Jannette that her father had helped her with a science project, and Jannette had gone straight to the teacher. Liza had had to do a whole new project, and none of them had trusted Jannette since.

That wasn't the only time she had gotten one of them in trouble, either. Chris had been summoned to the principal's office last year because Jannette claimed she had seen her smoking during recess.

Chris had really only been sucking on a lollipop, but no one had believed her until the principal made her go back and empty out her pockets and her desk — in front of everyone! It had been humiliating. Chris wanted to stay as far away from Jannette as possible this summer and for the rest of her life!

"Are you working here?" Chris asked in a weak voice.

"Sure am," Jannette answered pertly, tossing her silky blond hair over her shoulder. Chris wondered how two people could wear the same clothes and look so different. Chris's shorts were already rumpled and her polo shirt looked like she had borrowed it from her father. Jannette, on the other hand, looked as if she'd been born to model the outfit. The Palm Pavilion shirt fit her perfectly, showing off her slim, yet curvy figure. "What are you doing here?"

"Baby-sitting," Chris answered, glancing at Bruce.

"Well, what do you know!" cried Jannette. "So am I. We'll be spending the whole summer together, side by side. Isn't that great?"

"Great," Chris repeated. There was nothing she could think of that would spoil her chances with Bruce Johnson more completely than spending the summer standing next to tan, perky Jannette Sansibar. *Nothing*.

# Chapter Five

When the assignment sheet was posted, the words "Staff Meeting at Front Desk" were printed next to several names, including Liza's, Sam's and Chris's. They went to the front desk and waited there, along with two other girls, both of whom looked older than fourteen. One was a short girl who had long, red permed hair and wore a lot of makeup. The other was a petite, delicate girl with short, curly black hair and a Caribbean lilt to her low voice.

In a few minutes, Mr. Parker appeared, walking toward them in his usual rapid way. Beside him was Jannette Sansibar, holding a stack of papers and looking every bit as self-important as Mr. Parker himself.

"Greetings, ladies," he said. "Sorry for the delay, but Jannette and I were stapling together the last of my new booklets." Jannette handed each girl an inch-thick stack of papers stapled together. The cover sheet read, "Rules, Regulations and Helpful Hints for the Palm Pavilion Baby Sitters."

"Since this is the first year we have a baby-sitting program at the Palm Pavilion, I have compiled all my expectations into these few pages," Mr. Parker continued.

"Few!" Sam whispered. "This thing is thicker than last year's math book."

Mr. Parker shot her a withering glance, but said nothing. "I recommend that you commit this book to memory. In it you will find dress codes, behavior codes and hotel policies on such things as sick days, paydays and holidays."

"I wonder how many brownie points Jannette scored for helping with this thing," Chris whispered bitterly. As if things weren't bad enough, it was clear that Jannette was already manager's pet, just as she had managed to be teacher's pet every year in school. And it looked like she was going to be Bruce Johnson's favorite baby sitter, too — he hadn't been able to take his eyes off of her. It was too annoying for words!

Liza was about to whisper back that maybe they could find a way to lock Jannette in one of the linen closets for the summer, but she stopped herself. She was too stunned by the sight before her eyes to even speak. Instead, she jabbed Chris and Sam hard in the arms with her fingers.

"What?" Sam whispered irritably. By way of a reply, Liza just stood there with her jaw gaping open and continued jabbing. Sam followed her gaze and gasped.

Chris craned her neck to see what they were looking at. "Harrison Springfield!" she gasped.

Sure enough, walking into the lobby was the tall, blond actor. He wore a stylish, baggy white cotton suit. He stood with his hands in his pockets, surveying the lobby, and he looked as cool and handsome as he did in all of his movies. A ray of morning sunlight streamed down on him from the skylight, giving him an almost angelic glow.

"Oh, gosh, I'm going to faint," said Liza, holding tightly onto Sam's shoulders. Her knees buckled and her tanned face went ashen.

"Harrison Springfield," Chris whispered again, as if she were in a trance. "Winner of five Oscar nominations, three for Best Actor, two for Best Supporting Actor. Won the Best Actor award two years in a row. Winner of three Emmys and zillions of People's Choice Awards. The highest-paid actor in Hollywood, grossing seven-point-eight-million dollars last year alone. Hobbies include — "

Sam shoved her. "Snap out of it."

"Sorry," said Chris groggily. "Was I rambling? It's just that I know everything about Harrison Springfield. He's my favorite."

"Ladies!" Mr. Parker scolded. The two other girls had also noticed the actor, and even Jannette was staring at him. All six girls turned their attention back to Mr. Parker with dazed eyes, as if they were slowly being awakened from a dream.

"The clientele here at the Palm includes many

44

famous people, from all walks of life. We expect that you treat them with dignity and respect their privacy," Mr. Parker said in a serious tone.

All the girls nodded, except Liza. She was still staring at Harrison Springfield as he registered and left the lobby.

"That means *don't ogle the guests,* Miss Velez!" Mr. Parker said sternly. "Is that clear?"

Liza blinked at him. "Oh, sorry. Was I staring? Sorry," she sputtered.

"I have included a chapter titled 'Coping With Celebrities' in your booklet. I suggest you read it," Mr. Parker told the group. After a few more words about the rules, Mr. Parker asked Jannette to hand each girl a neatly-typed paper that listed her assignment for the day. "And if you should find yourself at a loss for something to do, come see me. We have no idlers at the Palm," he concluded.

As the girls were looking over their sheets, Mrs. Chan approached the group. "Mr. Parker," she said. "Mr. Springfield just called the front desk from his room. He requested that someone bring his son a coloring book and crayons from the gift shop. He's in room Seventeen-H."

"That's right, he has a son," Chris whispered to Liza. She had forgotten all about him. She made a mental promise to herself to study her Hollywood trivia book when she got home — she was definitely slipping!

Liza's hand shot up as if she were answering a

question in school. She waved it under Mr. Parker's nose. "I'd love to go. And I won't stare. I promise. Puh-*leeze,* Mr. Parker."

Mr. Parker shook his head. "I think Jannette would be better able to contain her enthusiasm," he said. He turned to Jannette, who smiled at him sweetly. "Tell the gift shop to put the coloring book and crayons on Mr. Springfield's tab."

"Yes, sir. Right away, sir," she chirped. Then, with an arrogant toss of her silky hair, she headed off toward the gift shop.

Mr. Parker clapped his hands brusquely. "You all have your assignments. Get to them!"

"I can't stand that girl," Liza complained when Mr. Parker had left. "Why did he let her go to Harrison Springfield's room instead of me?"

"Maybe because he figured she wouldn't tackle him," Sam answered. "She is a pain, though."

"I can't believe I'm in the same hotel with Harrison Springfield," sighed Chris. "I loved him in *Space Marauders.*"

"I think *Quest for the Stolen Pyramid* is his best," said Sam.

"He does almost all his own stunts," Chris informed them. "Isn't that amazing?"

"Who cares about that?" Liza said dreamily. "He does his own love scenes. That's what counts."

The girls quickly read their assignment sheets. "Hey, we're together," said Sam, comparing sheets with Chris. "We both have an assignment at the pool, helping the lifeguards run kiddie activities in the shallow end."

"Thank goodness you're going to be with me," said Chris, sighing with relief.

"Don't be so nervous," Sam assured her. "You'll be fine."

"I have to play checkers in the lobby with some kid named Hyram Schwartz," Liza told them, reading from her list. "That shouldn't be too hard."

"I have to take a kid named Remington Sheffield the Third on a picnic," groaned the girl with long red hair. "By the way, my name is Sunny Jones."

"I'm Lillian Greenwood," the other girl said.

Liza, Sam and Chris introduced themselves. "I guess we're the Palm Pavilion Baby Sitters," said Sam, liking the way the words sounded together.

"Maybe we should call ourselves the Palm-Palm Girls," mused Liza. "You know, I've always wanted to be one."

"Oh, please!" Chris groaned.

"Then I guess we'll have to work on our name," said Sunny, popping a pink bubblegum bubble. "We have all summer, right?"

"I'll let you know if I think of anything," Lillian promised. "Well, I'm off to the sandbox. See you later!"

The girls said good-bye and went off to their assignments. As her sheet instructed, Liza waited in the lobby at a table with an inlaid leather checkerboard. She kept a sharp eye out for little Hyram. He was supposed to arrive at nine-thirty, but at nine-

47

forty-five he still hadn't showed.

Liza was about to go to the desk to ask about Hyram when an old man came and sat down across from her. He was the oldest person Liza had ever seen. He was short and thin, with longish, wiry, white hair. His dry, wrinkled skin was splotched with brown age spots. Two beady, dark-brown eyes stared at Liza. She thought he must be at least one hundred years old.

"I'm sorry, sir," she said. "But I'm waiting here for a little boy."

"What?" shouted the man.

"A little boy," Liza shouted back. "A little boy named Hyram is going to play checkers with me here in a few minutes, so you'll have to move."

"You don't have to shout!" the man snapped. "I can hear you. And I'm not a little kid."

Liza gasped. "You mean *you're* Hyram?"

"Mr. Schwartz to you," the man said sourly.

"Sorry," Liza apologized.

The man opened the box of checkers with surprisingly steady hands. "Come on, let's play. That's what they pay you for, isn't it?"

"Not exactly," said Liza. "I'm a baby sitter."

"I've been told I act like a big baby sometimes, so you're stuck with me."

Liza wasn't sure whether or not he was kidding, but she set up the pieces and they began the game. She soon discovered that Mr. Schwartz played by his own rules. When she tried to tell him he wasn't

48

supposed to move all his pieces forward and backward, he just glared at her. But if *she* tried to move her pieces in both directions, he slapped her hand with his bony fingers.

She was scheduled to play with Mr. Schwartz for two hours. She sighed and settled in, resigned to her fate. When Mr. Schwartz had won the twelfth game in a row, Liza told him she needed a two-minute break. She stood and stretched and looked around the lobby.

She stopped in mid-stretch when she saw Jannette cutting across the lobby holding the hand of a small boy with tousled blond hair. He wore a pair of trunks and a cotton jacket, and held a towel — all of which were red with small monkeys on them. He held a large red pail full of shovels and other beach equipment. Behind Jannette and the boy were Harrison Springfield and his tall, slim, blond wife, the actress Moira Alezandro.

"Well, are you going to play, or what?" grumbled the old man.

It wasn't fair! Here she was, stuck inside with the world's oldest grouch, while Jannette was out there basking in the sunlight with the Springfield family.

She watched them walk down to a lower level and disappear out the back door. "Set 'em up, Mr. Schwartz," she said glumly, sitting back down at the table.

Outside, Chris and Sam grabbed one another's

arms when they saw Jannette and the Springfields coming toward them at the pool. Harrison and his wife went left, toward the beach, and their son stayed with Jannette.

"Rats," said Chris. "I was hoping he'd stick around."

"Hey, look," said Sam, nodding her head toward the far end of the pool where Bruce Johnson was setting out beach chairs. "What a bod."

"He *is* gorgeous," said Chris. "Too bad he'll never look at me twice. Not with Jannette around."

"Don't give up so easily," said Sam. "Jannette is kind of a bubble-brain."

"Yeah, but she's a beautiful bubble-brain," replied Chris.

Jannette and Harrison Springfield's son joined the group of seven kids who were waiting for the activities to begin. A small woman wearing a green tank suit approached Sam, Chris and Jannette. She had a taut, athletic body and one long, dark braid hanging down her back. "I'm Julie, the head lifeguard," she introduced herself. "From now on, bring bathing suits with you for pool activities. You never know when you'll have to jump in."

"I have mine on already," said Jannette, lifting up her shirt to show that she was wearing a blue bathing suit under her shorts and shirt.

"It figures," Chris muttered under her breath to Sam.

"Okay, everybody ready for kiddie water volley-ball?" asked Julie.

The girls nodded. Julie then instructed them to keep a sharp eye out on the kids. "We have eight today. Make sure you see eight heads at all times." She then assigned them to different stations along the pool to keep watch.

"I hope we get a lot of these assignments," said Sam as she and Chris walked toward their spots. "That way Julie will get to know me and she'll hire me for a lifeguard job in a few years."

Julie got all the kids into the shallow end of the kiddie pool and split them into two teams. The children ranged in age from about four to seven. She put the little children in the middle and the taller ones behind. The pool was shallow enough so that all the kids could stand on the bottom while they played. Julie tossed a floating rope into the water and lined it up between the teams. Then they began a game of volleyball, using a large red-and-yellow striped beach ball.

A loud wail rang out almost immediately. It was Harrison Springfield's son. "Jason didn't really want to do this!" Jannette called to Julie.

Julie waded out toward the crying boy and spoke a few words to him that seemed to calm him. Soon everyone was in place and Julie blew a whistle for the game to start again.

Chris stood and watched the children as they splashed one another and tried to get the ball. They looked so cool and happy. It was almost ten o'clock but the sun was already blazing down. *I'm going to fry out here,* thought fair-skinned Chris, even though she had put on an extra-heavy dose of sunscreen that morning.

She squinted and peered across the pool at Bruce Johnson, who was hosing down the cement area around the beach chairs. His back was to her and the sunlight made the back of his white polo shirt seem to shine. How broad his shoulders were! And his tan legs were all muscle.

Chris imagined walking with him by the pool. She pictured him laughing at something very witty that she had said. Then, in her mind, she saw him wrap his arms around her and pull her to him, kissing her sweetly on the lips.

A splash of cold water from the pool brought her back to reality. The game was going at full speed as the children batted the ball back and forth.

Feeling guilty for having been daydreaming on the job, Chris quickly took a head count. One, two, three, four, five, six, seven. She counted again. Still only seven. Panicked, her eyes darted from child to child.

Jason Springfield was missing!

# Chapter Six

Without a second thought, Chris jumped into the pool and began thrashing around, looking for the boy who, she was sure, had sunk beneath the water. She held her nose and went under, keeping her eyes open. She saw a foggy landscape of short, sturdy legs standing firmly on the pool's blue cement bottom, but no Jason Springfield.

There was a split second when she envisioned what she was looking for — a small boy unconscious at the bottom of the pool. The very idea sent a chill through her.

Then she heard a shrill whistle and came to the surface to find Julie staring at her with wide, questioning eyes. In fact, everyone in the pool was looking at her.

"Jason Springfield," she explained breathlessly. "He's missing."

Julie looked at her and pointed. Chris followed the

direction of Julie's finger and saw Jason in the water with Jannette. He was paddling around happily, wearing a snorkeling mask and flippers.

"Oh," Chris said, gulping.

"Didn't you see me stop the game and say he could go snorkel with Jannette?" asked Julie in a calm but clearly annoyed tone of voice.

Chris didn't want to admit that she'd been daydreaming. "I . . . I . . . I guess it slipped my mind," she stammered. "Sorry."

"Your heart was in the right place, but pay attention next time. Besides, *I'm* the lifeguard around here," said Julie crossly.

Chris climbed out of the pool. Her waterlogged sneakers felt like they weighed a ton, and she was suddenly self-conscious about the way her wet shorts and shirt were sticking to her. She looked around quickly and her eyes met Bruce's. From across the pool, he had witnessed the entire scene. He smiled and gave her the thumbs-up sign. Of course, she knew he was teasing. There was nothing thumbs-up about what she'd just done. There was nothing thumbs-up about making an idiot of yourself, being scolded in front of everyone, and then standing there red-faced and sopping wet.

"Miss Brown!" came the piercing and already too-familiar voice of Mr. Parker. Chris turned and realized he was charging toward her from the far end of the pool. She squinted into the sun and saw that he was not smiling. "Miss Brown," he repeated in a low, menacing voice. "My day is full of much stress. There are continual problems in the kitchen, in the restaurants, among the guests and staff. Should you decide to become one more source of stress in my life . . . " He leaned in close to Chris and raised the level of his voice, " . . . then I shall be forced to fire you. Do you understand?"

Chris stepped back and heard her soaked sneakers squish. "Yes, Mr. Parker," she answered. "I just thought that the poor kid had gone under and — " The look on Mr. Parker's face told her that he was not interested in hearing her story. "Never mind. I'm very sorry."

Mr. Parker nodded sharply and walked off. "I'll be keeping my eye on you, Miss Brown," he said over his shoulder.

Chris smiled at him lamely. "Great," she muttered to herself.

"You're certainly starting off with a bang, Christine," Sam teased her.

Chris twisted the water from the bottom of her polo shirt and looked over at Sam. Her friend smiled consolingly and shrugged her shoulders as if to say, "What can you do? These things happen." It seemed to Chris that nothing ruffled Sam. But, then again, Sam wasn't embarrassing herself every time she turned around.

Liza, Chris and Sam met at the front desk after their shift was over. "Do you believe they made me play checkers all day with a thousand-year-old man!" Liza complained. "I asked Mrs. Chan about it and she reminded me that when there aren't enough kids to baby-sit, we're expected to do whatever is needed to make the guests happy. But why me?"

"It doesn't sound like it was *that* bad," said Sam. "Why are you so steamed?"

"Oh, it just burns me that Jannette spent all day with the Springfields," Liza complained. "She isn't worthy of hanging out with a star like Harrison Springfield. She probably couldn't care less if he put her in his next movie or not. The whole experience is totally wasted on her."

"What would you do if you got the job?" Sam asked.

"I'd make sure he noticed my star quality, that's for sure." Liza rotated her neck in a circle. It was stiff from hunching over a checkerboard all morning. "I've just got to meet him. I'm determined to do it, no matter what."

A maid passed them, rolling a cart full of fresh towels. She parked the cart and walked over to the soda machine at the very front of the hotel. "Even the maid gets to meet Harrison Springfield," said Chris. "I bet he was in his room when she cleaned it today."

Liza's eyes brightened. "You just gave me a great idea," she said. "Follow me."

Chris and Sam walked behind Liza as she headed for the cart. With one swift motion, Liza scooped three towels from the top of the towel pile and headed out of the lobby. She kept walking until she was in one of the long hallways that led to the guests' rooms. Then she glanced over her shoulder and handed Chris and Sam each a towel.

"What are you up to?" Sam asked suspiciously.

"You'll see," Liza answered. "Come on." She led them down the hall to a bank of elevators. They got into the next car that was going up and Liza pressed the button marked seventeen.

They got out at the seventeenth floor and discovered that there were only three rooms on the whole floor.

"I guess the superduper deluxe rooms are up here," Sam said, awed by the luxury of her surroundings.

"Seventeen-H. That's where Mrs. Chan said Harrison Springfield was staying," said Liza, folding the towel neatly over her arm.

"Excuse me, but I don't quite get this plan," said Chris. "What are we doing with these towels?"

Liza looked at her scornfully, as if the answer should be obvious. "We're going to pretend we're the maids coming to change the towels. We've got our official hotel shirts on. I think we can pull it off."

"What good is that going to do?" asked Sam.

"We'll get to meet Harrison Springfield, stupid," Liza explained.

Chris and Sam exchanged worried glances.

"Don't you want to meet a famous star?" Liza pressed. "What are you, chicken?"

"We're not chicken. We just don't want to get fired," Chris explained. She had come close enough already.

"There's no way you're going to get fired. How could anyone ever catch us?" Liza insisted. "We'll only be in there for a minute or two. It's not like Mr. Parker's going to walk by on the seventeenth floor."

"That's true," Sam agreed. "Let's do it."

Liza walked up to the door marked 17-H with Chris and Sam following close behind her. She rapped boldly and waited. Chris giggled nervously, but Liza turned and silenced her with a stern look. "You have to *believe* that you're a maid, otherwise your audience won't believe you. I read that in a book on acting," she said to Chris.

They stood, shifting from foot to foot anxiously for a few more seconds, and then the door opened. Moira Alezandro stood before them, her long blond curls flowing freely over her shoulders. She wore a white bikini bathing suit with a flowing, flowered coverup draped over her shoulders. In her hand she held the pages of what appeared to be a movie script. She looked beautiful, but older than in her movies. "Yes?" she asked in a low, melodious voice.

"We've come with fresh towels," said Liza, trying to sound very official.

"Our towels are fine, but I suppose one can never have too many fresh towels," she said absently, as if her mind were on something else. She threw the script on a chair. "I was on my way out," she said.

"No problem," Liza told her. "We'll be sure to lock up when we leave."

The actress looked at the girls skeptically for a

moment, then picked up a large straw beach bag with straw flowers sewn into it and left the room.

"I don't believe this place," cried Sam, gazing around at the two-bedroom suite once they were inside the living room. Modern white sofas and smoked-glass tables stood on a thick green carpet. Sliding glass doors formed two sides of the corner room and opened to a wraparound terrace overlooking the ocean. To their right, up two steps, was an elegant dining area with a large, octagonal table also of smoked glass. The bedrooms and bath were off to the left of the dining area.

"This is bigger than my whole house and there's not even a kitchen in here," Chris observed with a loud sigh.

"Get a look at this!" Liza called out from the spacious black- and gold-tiled bathroom. On a platform was a round whirlpool tub, and behind it was a glassed-in shower and steam room. On the far wall was another picture window with a full view of the ocean.

"Do you think these fixtures are solid gold?" Sam asked as she turned on the water in the sink. The golden fixture was shaped like a conch shell.

"I don't know," said Chris, "but this is the most beautiful faucet I've ever seen." She patted the head of the golden seahorse whose mouth sprayed water into the sink.

The girls left the bathroom and stuck their heads into the smaller of the two bedrooms. "This kid sure likes monkeys," said Chris. The entire room was covered with pictures of monkeys and apes of all kinds. There were posters and drawings everywhere.

"The kid hasn't even been here a day," Sam noted. "He must bring this stuff with him wherever he goes."

"He even had on a monkey-print bathing suit this morning," Liza recalled.

They moved into the master bedroom with its king-sized bed and private, glassed-in balcony. "This is where Harrison Springfield sleeps," Liza observed with a loud sigh.

"It's kind of warm in this room," Chris observed.

"We'd better get out of here," said Sam.

"I guess so," Liza agreed reluctantly. The three girls headed for the door. Liza stopped and picked up the script Moira Alezandro had thrown on the chair. "Just let me see if there's a part here for me," she said, scanning the dialogue quickly. "Oh, neat, this is about two teachers in a girls' boarding school. There's definitely a part here for — "

Liza was stopped short by a sharp rap on the door. The girls looked at one another in panic. The next sound they heard was the jangle of keys in the door. Without a word, Liza and Sam bolted straight for the bathroom.

Chris stood for a moment, paralyzed with fear. She didn't see any good hiding places. The door opened before she could make a move and she found herself staring right at Mr. Parker. Behind him stood a man in brown coveralls holding a large metal toolbox.

Mr. Parker's eyes widened when he saw Chris. "The air-conditioning problem is in the master bedroom," he instructed the man, who went in to work on it.

Without meaning to, Chris backed away a few steps from Mr. Parker.

"May I ask what you are doing here, Miss Brown?" Mr. Parker inquired in a voice that was eerily calm.

Chris heard a noise in the bathroom and automatically flinched. She quickly tried to regain her composure, since Mr. Parker was staring into her eyes. If she looked too nervous, she could easily give her friends away. "I . . . umm . . . uh . . . I . . . " she stammered. "I just came up here to see if the Springfields needed anything done for them before I left for the day," she lied desperately.

Mr. Parker continued to stare at her.

"Just trying to go that extra mile," she added, giggling nervously. "You know, give that little bit of extra attention guests expect from the Palm Pavilion."

"So what are you doing in here all alone?" he asked.

Chris's mind went blank. All she could do was blink at Mr. Parker.

"Could it be you were snooping?" suggested Mr. Parker, his voice slowly rising to a shrill pitch. "Could it be you were violating the privacy that these people pay us vast quantities of money to respect? Hmmm?"

Chris could feel a warm blush forming on her cheeks. She clasped her hands in front of her to stop them from shaking. "I just wanted to see the room," she told him. "I brought up a towel and Mrs. Springfield let me in. I was just looking around. Honestly."

Just then there was a loud clatter as if something had been knocked over. Mr. Parker looked up. *That does it,* thought Chris. He would go into the bathroom and discover Liza and Sam. Then he'd really blow his stack.

Chris sucked in her breath. "Be careful in there," Mr. Parker called to the repairman. "You break it, you buy it."

"I didn't touch a thing!" the man called back in an annoyed tone.

Chris exhaled. The noise seemed to have broken Mr. Parker's concentration. "Get out of here, Miss Brown," he said gruffly. "I consider myself a fair and patient man, but you have been working here only one day and you already have two strikes against you. One more infraction — even the tiniest bending of the rules — and your employment will be terminated. Do we understand one another?"

"Yes, sir, Mr. Parker," she answered, backing toward the door. "Thank you for the second chance. Really, thank you."

"If anything is damaged or missing from this room, I will consider that strike three."

"Yes. I mean no, nothing is missing. I didn't touch a thing," she assured him. Chris stood by the open door, wondering if she was free to leave.

"Don't just stand there," he snapped.

"Yes, sir." She scooted out the door and closed it quietly behind her.

She leaned against the wall and caught her breath. That was close. She'd made it out of there in one piece.

But now, she wondered what she should do next. She couldn't just go home — not with Sam and Liza still trapped inside. She had to come up with a plan to get them out of there — fast!

# Chapter Seven

Chris hung back at the end of the hallway, near the fire exit door. She didn't see any place where she could hide while she waited for Sam and Liza. The fire stairs would be her only escape if Mr. Parker came out of the room.

*I feel like I've been waiting out here forever,* she thought. *What's going on? Why don't Sam and Liza come out? I could die of old age standing here.*

She couldn't even get comfortable and sit on the floor or slouch against the wall as she might have ordinarily. She was too worried that Mr. Parker would suddenly appear, find her hanging around, and scream, "Strike three!" loud enough for the entire hotel to hear.

*I wonder if Mr. Parker found them,* Chris mused. *He's probably giving them the third degree right now. Well, if they get caught maybe we'll all be fired. Then we'll be able to loaf around the rest of the summer, just like I'd planned!*

But even that pleasant idea wasn't enough to make Chris relax. There was always the possibility that Mr. Parker would do something drastic, like call their parents — or even the police. After all, they *had* made their way into a superstar's room under false pretenses. It wasn't breaking and entering but it had to be trespassing, or unlawful loitering, at least. Chris knew these terms from all the police shows she watched, but she wasn't sure which were punishable with jail sentences. *Oh, great. Now I'll never make it to the ninth grade.*

She pictured the three of them wearing plain gray dresses and bunking together in some detention center for juvenile delinquent girls. Naturally, Chris saw this as a TV series. She heard an announcer's deep voice speaking over the opening credits: "What started as an innocent lark ended in disaster. For sneaking into the room of a famous movie star, these girls will now spend the rest of their teen years as prisoners. Welcome to *Three in a Cell . . . .*"

Suddenly a quick rap on the door behind her made Chris's heart leap. She jumped away from the door. Who could possibly be on the fire stairs? A thief? No, a thief wouldn't knock. The police?

Cautiously Chris pulled open the door — and came face to face with Bruce Johnson. She blinked, thinking that maybe she was seeing things. But she wasn't.

"What are you doing here?" Bruce asked, stepping

into the hallway. His face was red and he was breathing hard from the effort of climbing the stairs. In his hand was a small roll of heavy silver tape.

"Umm . . . it's a long story," Chris answered. "Why did you come up the stairs?"

"The elevator doors aren't closing right, so they're working on them. Mr. Parker said the air-conditioning guy needed this tape right away. Man, for an expensive hotel, this place is falling apart," he said.

Chris saw that he had very long, dark eyelashes and a perfect, kind of slightly turned-up, nose. She'd never noticed that he had a slight dimple in his chin.

"Wow! You climbed up seventeen flights of stairs?" she asked, genuinely impressed.

"Two steps at a time," he told her proudly. "It builds up my legs for surfing. I almost croaked when I found out the door was locked, though. Good thing you were here."

"Yes," Chris agreed, feeling herself begin to melt as she gazed up into his blue eyes. No wonder his legs were so wonderfully muscular.

"You look like you've pretty much dried off after your dunk in the pool," he said smiling.

*Do not turn red,* Chris commanded herself as she felt the tips of her ears start to tingle warmly. "I really goofed," she said, trying to sound as if she thought the whole episode was funny. "But I thought the kid had drowned."

"If he *had* gone under, you would have done the right thing," he said. "Better to be safe than sorry."

66

"That's what I thought," said Chris. She'd been worried that a boy as good-looking as Bruce might be stuck-up. But he was as nice as she'd hoped. He made the whole humiliating incident at the pool seem okay. If he only knew that the reason she hadn't noticed Jason Springfield leave the volleyball game was because she was busy staring at him! "Mr. Parker sure was angry, though," she added.

"Ah, that guy's always steamed about something."

Chris smiled at him. "My name is Chris Brown, by the way."

"I'm Bruce Johnson."

Chris had to stop herself from saying that she already knew his name. That would have been very uncool. "I think I remember you from school," she said, trying to sound casual.

He looked at her intently, but nothing seemed to register. "What grade are you in?" he asked.

There was no sense pretending to be older than she was. There was only one grammar school, one middle school and one high school in Bonita Beach. "I just got out of eighth grade," she said.

"Are you fourteen yet?"

"Uh-huh." That was only a small lie. She'd be fourteen in three weeks.

"Good thing," he told her. "Parker's going to ask you for working papers eventually, and you can't get them until you're fourteen. That girl Jannette was telling me she turned fourteen last week, so she just made it."

*Great,* thought Chris. Now, on top of everything, she was going to have to stall Mr. Parker about working papers for three weeks. *If* she lasted that long.

"Jannette must be in the same class as you," Bruce observed.

Chris's heart sank. The dreamy look on Bruce's face told her immediately that Jannette was a subject of great interest to him.

"You must know her," he went on when Chris didn't respond.

"Sure," said Chris. Bruce looked at her expectantly, as though he was hoping she'd tell him something more about Jannette. "She's okay," Chris said, answering his unspoken question as dully as possible. What else could she say? She didn't want to talk about how pretty Jannette was, but she didn't want to seem mean and petty, either, by telling him how she really felt about her least favorite classmate.

"She and I have been assigned to take the little kiddies on a trip to the zoo in a couple of days," he told her. "I think we still need more baby sitters. Why don't you sign up? Mrs. Chan's got the sheet at the front desk."

"I will. Sounds like fun," Chris said brightly. Maybe she had a chance with him, after all. He had invited her to come along on the trip. That meant that at least he didn't think she was some kind of a jerk.

"I'd better deliver this tape," he said. "The air-conditioning repair guy needs it and Parker kept screaming over the house phone that he's paying him by the hour."

Mr. Parker. For a few delightful minutes, Chris had almost forgotten about him. "You'd better get in there," she agreed.

He headed toward the door and then turned back to her. "You never told me what you're doing up here."

"Umm . . . just hoping to get a look at Harrison Springfield, is all," Chris answered sheepishly.

"You'd better not stick around. Bugging the rich and famous is a big crime in Parker's book."

"Thanks for the advice," she said. She backed into the fire door. "I'm going."

"Okay," he said, looking as if he were waiting for her to leave.

"I'm going," she assured him with a nervous giggle. "Just give me a minute to get ready for all those steps."

"Okay," he said. "Parker might come out here any second."

"I know that. Thanks." She waved him on. "You'd better not keep him waiting."

"Yeah," he agreed and knocked on the door. Chris flattened herself against the fire door as the door to 17-H opened and Bruce stepped into the room.

"Come on, Liza and Sam," she whispered. Time was running out. If Mr. Parker didn't catch her, then Bruce would come out again and think she was an oddball for still hanging around. Still, she couldn't bring herself to just take off, with her friends trapped inside.

A few seconds later, the door to the Springfields' room opened slowly. Liza and Sam slipped through on tiptoe and closed the door quietly behind them. Sam ran to the elevator and pounded the down button.

"In here," Chris whispered, holding open the fire door. "The elevator isn't working."

Liza and Sam raced through the door. Chris followed and shut the door behind her. When they had run down a few flights of stairs, they stopped on a landing and Liza and Sam exploded with laughter.

Chris looked at them with questioning eyes. "Mr. Parker didn't catch you, did he?"

"Oh, my gosh. Oh, my gosh," Liza panted, leaning against the stair railing. "I thought I was going to die. Imagine if Harrison Springfield had come back and found the two of us standing in his shower!"

"I almost fainted when Mr. Parker came in to wash his hands," Sam said, gasping with laughter. "I can't believe he didn't see us."

"Thank goodness that shower had such thick, bubbled glass," said Liza.

"How did you get out?" asked Chris.

"When it got real quiet in the living room, we crept out and saw that they were all in the bedroom looking at the air conditioner. It looked like the coast was clear, so we made a beeline for the door," Sam explained. She and Liza looked at one another and burst out laughing all over again.

"You guys might think it's funny," said Chris, "but

70

*I'm* the one who got caught. Mr. Parker said that if I goof one more time I'm out."

Sam and Liza stopped laughing. "Sorry," said Liza sincerely. "I'm the one who dragged you into this."

"You're a good pal to wait out here all this time for us," Sam added.

"Well," said Chris. "Something good did happen. Bruce Johnson came up here and he actually talked to me. It turns out he's really nice — not to mention unbelievably cute."

"We *thought* that was him in the room with Mr. Parker and the repair guy," Sam said.

"But we didn't want to stick around to make sure," added Liza.

"He invited me to go on a trip to the zoo that the hotel is running," Chris told them. "You guys have to sign up, too. I don't have the nerve to go alone."

"Don't you want to be alone with him?" Sam asked.

"Jannette's going, too," she told them. "I'd feel too dumb if it was just me, him and Jannette."

"All right," Liza agreed. "I probably owe you a favor for getting you into trouble with Mr. Parker."

"It might be fun," said Sam. "I'll sign up."

"Thanks," said Chris. "Well, let's get going. We still have fourteen flights to go, and we'd better get out of this stairwell before Parker comes down."

"I'll race you!" Sam cried, starting down the stairs.

"I think I'll go slowly," Chris answered. "The way my day is going, I don't want to take any more risks!"

# *Chapter Eight*

Chris stopped her bike in front of her house. "This sure was some first day of work," said Sam, coming to a stop beside her.

"It sure was," agreed Liza, gliding in with her legs up on the handlebars of her bike. "I hope Harrison Springfield is there again tomorrow." She dropped her legs down and let her feet drag along the cement. "And I hope I don't have to play checkers with that Hyram Schwartz again. What a grouch — *and* a cheater."

"I'm pooped." Chris sighed. "I'm glad I'm not scheduled to work tomorrow."

"But we are — bright and early," Sam complained as she pushed off on her bike.

Liza grimaced. "I don't know how bright it is to get up that early, but what can we do?" She waved to Chris as she and Sam pedaled away.

Chris waved back and then stood for a minute,

looking at her small, yellow wooden house with its neat white shutters and trimmed green lawn. She looked at the narrow dirt driveway that ran along the side of her house and saw that her father's old blue Chevy was there. Her mother was probably home from school by now, too. Somehow she just couldn't bring herself to go in. They'd want to know how her first day at work had been, what she had done — and more importantly, *how* she had done. They would hang on her every word and say they were sure she was the best baby sitter the Palm had ever known.

Chris often wished that she wasn't an only child. If she had a brother or a sister, then maybe her parents wouldn't be so intensely interested in everything she did. She knew that would never happen, though. They'd had her when they were in their late thirties and now they were too old to have any more children. Chris had heard some kids complain that their parents didn't pay enough attention to them. That wasn't Chris's problem. She was suffering from an overload of attention!

Chris's parents were sweet and she knew they loved her, but at the moment she wasn't quite ready for their enthusiasm, not when the day had been so crummy. She couldn't bear for them to be all excited about yet another thing she was going to fail at. And she couldn't talk to them about the one thing that had gone right — talking to Bruce Johnson. They'd simply say, "That's nice," and move on to the next subject.

Needing time to think, Chris pushed off on her bike and headed in the opposite direction from town. She pedaled through the fancy part of Bonita Beach where the hedges grew high, partly hiding from view the big white houses with their graceful, two-tiered porches. The air around her was sweet with the smell of hibiscus flowers.

It took almost ten minutes to get onto the dirt road which led to the best beaches. Chris turned at a small, weathered wooden sign with the words *Castaway Cove* burned into it, then walked her bike along the rocky, narrow path that cut through a patch of tall trees.

Soon the smell of salt air and the sound of crashing waves surrounded her. She leaned her bike against a tree. She wasn't worried about anyone stealing it. Not many people came to the cove and it just wasn't the kind of place you would come to if you were looking for trouble. It was just a sandy little horseshoe-shaped patch of beach that the water had carved out of the land.

Chris made her way down the steep hill that led to the beach. When she got to the bottom, she removed her sneakers and peeled off her socks. The warm sand felt good between her toes. It was almost five o'clock. There were still several hours before sunset, but the gentle bluish cast of late afternoon was already beginning to set in. She loved this spot, especially around suppertime when it was nearly always deserted.

A warm breeze was blowing off the ocean. Chris shut her eyes and lifted her face to it. Her thoughts drifted and she let the peacefulness of the spot engulf her. For a moment there was no Mr. Parker, or Jannette Sansibar or Palm Pavilion Hotel. There was only the sound of the ocean.

She opened her eyes and looked out at the sea. Two large pelicans were flying over the water, looking for their supper. She never tired of watching them dive straight down into the water to snatch fish, and then return to the surface with their catch in their bills.

After a while, she got up and waded into the surf. The swirling water around her ankles and calves refreshed her. She decided to take a walk along the shoreline, kicking her feet in the water as she walked.

*I can't get over the Palm Pavilion,* she thought. *It's like something out of a movie.* Chris had always known that the hotel was like another world in the middle of Bonita Beach, where rich people relaxed and town people worked. It was, as Liza had said, a lot like the idea of heaven — another perfect place that people said existed, but that never really touched your day-to-day life. It had never touched hers, anyway, until now.

*I'm not even sure I like it that much. It's so fancy, it's intimidating.* The picture of Harrison Springfield's golden bathroom fixtures stuck in her mind. *Gold! In the bathroom!* It was too strange . . . .

Chris walked along, lost in her thoughts of the

hotel, when she was suddenly startled by a fluttering in the palms to her right. She'd roused a snowy white heron, who now flapped his amazingly wide wings and seemed to drift effortlessly up into the sky. He swooped in front of her, gliding on the currents of air, breathtakingly graceful for such a large bird.

It was times like these that Chris felt incredibly lucky to be living in Bonita Beach all year round — instead of being a tourist there. Her mother sometimes spoke fondly of her childhood, which she had spent in different parts of the Midwest. She talked about the majestic mountains and lakes. But Chris knew she wouldn't have liked it. She'd been born in Bonita Beach and the ocean was so much a part of her that she couldn't imagine ever being away from it. The ocean tides seemed to pull all the bad, sad feelings out of her, and then send her feelings back to her, clean and new.

No matter how dazzling the Palm Pavilion was, Chris knew that she'd never want to trade it for the pleasure of walking along the beach and being surprised by a white heron. All the golden faucets in the world could never replace that.

Chris rounded the bend in the cove. On the other side was a stretch of straight, white sandy beach, where the water wasn't sheltered by the rocks and sand banks of the cove. It was rougher, and the waves were much higher.

A large flock of pelicans hovered in the sky, dipping into the ocean frequently. Chris knew they must have found a spot rich with fish.

Just past the flock she saw three boys on surfboards riding the waves. She walked a few yards closer to get a better look at them. The vivid reds, yellows and greens of their boards and knee-length bathing trunks stood out against the blue ocean and sky. She could hear them whoop with excitement when a large wave came and scooped them up, carrying them along on its curling crest.

Chris admired the way they controlled their boards, balancing perfectly. Sometimes she thought boys were just stupid, thick-headed idiots who made noise and said dumb things. There were other times, though, times like this, when their wildness and strength thrilled her.

One of the boys rode a wave most of the way into shore. As he hopped off his board and waded the rest of the way in, Chris realized it was Bruce. He saw her standing there and waved.

"Hi!" he called, pulling his board up and carrying it under one arm. He flipped his blond hair back out of his eyes and smiled.

"Hi!" she shouted back above the roar of the surf. Bruce walked up toward her on the beach and dropped his board onto the sand. They stared awkwardly at one another for a moment.

The other two boys rode the next wave in to shore.

Chris felt self-conscious about the fact that she was still wearing the same shirt and shorts he'd seen her in all day — the ones she had jumped into the pool in, too. "I was just taking a walk," she explained. "I'd better be going — it's almost time to get home for dinner." Chris wanted to kick herself — what a babyish thing to say!

"I'll see you at work," he said. "So long."

"Yeah, see you." With a quick wave, Chris turned and headed back toward the cove. She knew that although the spectacular wealth of the hotel didn't impress her, the place held something — or, rather, some*one* — that she wanted very much to be close to.

# Chapter Nine

Since Chris wasn't scheduled to work the next day, she spent it daydreaming about what she would say to Bruce when she saw him again — and worrying that Mr. Parker would fire her on the spot when *he* saw *her*.

On Friday, Liza, Sam and Chris rode to work together and punched the time clock once again. One look at the schedule posted on the kitchen wall gave Chris some good news and some bad news. The good news was that Mr. Parker had called in sick. The bad news was that Bruce wasn't scheduled to work that day. Neither was Jannette.

For a fleeting moment Chris imagined the two of them surfing together, Jannette's perfectly styled, white-blond hair blowing as she stood in front of Bruce on the same board. Jannette was the kind of girl who would look terrific on a surfboard. When Chris tried to imagine herself on a board with Bruce all she could see was a realistic picture of what would happen. She envisioned herself slipping off the board, coming up looking like a drowned rat, and being so hopeless that Bruce would give up and surf off, leaving her to flounder in the water all by herself.

"Hey, get a load of this," called Liza, reading off a sheet of paper tacked to the wall next to the work schedule. It was the list of food specials for all three restaurants. "Today's special is 'The Bonita Bonito.' It's bonito fish in the chef's special sauce. What a stupid name. I wonder who thought up — "

Sam noticed Chef Alleyne glaring at Liza and poked her in the arm. Liza turned and swallowed hard. She didn't like the look on his round face, or the sharp cleaver he clutched in his hand. She gave him a thin smile and shot out of the kitchen, followed by Chris and Sam.

The rest of the day went quickly. The Springfields were not around. When the girls asked, Mrs. Chan told them that the actor and his family had left for a scuba-diving trip first thing in the morning. Liza was assigned to play checkers with Mr. Schwartz once again. She was surprised to hear that he'd specially requested her. Chris and Sam were once again assigned to pool duty with Julie.

"This was a pretty easy day," said Sam, when they rode home that afternoon.

"A boring day, you mean," grumbled Liza. "I'm supposed to baby-sit for babies, not grouchy old men."

80

"He's got to leave eventually," said Sam, riding alongside her.

"I have the horrible feeling that the guy lives there," Liza replied as she came to a stop at a red light.

"He must be pretty rich, then," said Sam. "I saw a rate card, and the cheapest room there is two hundred and fifty dollars a day."

"Wow!" cried Chris, coming up behind them, red-faced. She had been pedaling hard to catch up with Liza and Sam. "Two hundred and fifty dollars!"

"Those are the small rooms that don't even face the water," added Sam. "Maybe old Hyram is a multimillionaire."

"I don't care," Liza said as she pushed off again when the light turned green. "It's not fair that I have to spend the whole time inside with him."

"Tomorrow will be better," Chris assured her. "I don't think Hyram is going to want to go to the zoo with us."

Liza smiled. "That's true. No Hyram. No Mr. Parker. It should be fun."

"And Chris gets to spend the day with Brucie baby," Sam teased.

"Bruce *and* Jannette," Chris reminded her sourly.

"Oh, well, you can't have everything," quipped Sam.

That night after dinner, Chris washed her hair and blow-dried it, carefully tucking under the ends with a rounded brush. She covered her face with a mint-green face pack. When she'd washed that off, she made sure to cover the blemishes on her chin with medicated cream. Later she actually got out the iron and tried to press some Jannette-like crispness into her official staff polo shirt and her favorite pair of flowered shorts.

Her father stood in front of her, wiping his wire-rimmed glasses over and over as he watched her. "What's the matter with your glasses?" asked Chris.

"I must be seeing things," he answered. "For a minute I thought you were ironing."

Chris gave an exasperated sigh, but then smiled despite herself. "I *am* ironing, Dad. I have to look neat for work."

"I'm very impressed," he said, settling down on the couch with the local newspaper. "You must really like this job, then."

Chris had managed to duck her parents' questions up until now. "It's okay," she answered.

He opened his mouth as if he were about to ask another question, then thought better of it. "Good," he said simply, and went back to his paper. Chris was pleasantly surprised. It was probably part of some sort of psychological plan her parents had agreed upon — they were always reading books on child psychology — but she was glad her father had dropped the subject.

The next day, when Liza and Sam came to pick her

up, Chris was dressed in an old T-shirt and a pair of baggy gym shorts. She had her good clothes in a bag. She was determined not to start out the trip to the zoo in a wrinkled shirt, damp with perspiration.

After they had punched in and Chris had changed quickly in the women employees' locker room, she headed to the front desk, where the group was supposed to meet with Mrs. James, the woman who conducted many of the hotel-sponsored children's outings.

Bruce and Jannette were already there, waiting. Chris didn't like the admiring way Bruce was gazing at Jannette, but she decided not to let it get her down. "Hi, Bruce, Jannette," she said cheerfully. "Ready for a big day at the zoo?"

"Sure am," chirped Jannette.

"I have some bad news, though," said Bruce. "Mrs. James has that cold that's going around, so rather than cancel the trip, Mr. Parker is coming along."

"Oh, no!" Liza and Sam exclaimed simultaneously.

Jannette put her hands on her hips and pursed her lips disapprovingly. "Now come on, you two, don't be that way about Mr. Parker. He's a nice man."

"Are you crazy?" sputtered Chris. "He's a tyrant."

Sam nudged Chris's leg with her sneaker and pulled her away from the group. "Don't say anything else," she warned in a whisper. "You know Jannette. She'll definitely tell Parker what you said. Remember, we're dealing with the infamous school spy."

"But this isn't school," Chris objected.

"That doesn't mean she won't act the same way," reasoned Sam. "Be careful what you say around her."

"I guess you're right," Chris agreed as they rejoined the group. Two boys who looked about seven or eight years old had arrived, and a little girl with blond curls was there, holding her mother's hand.

Chris looked toward Mr. Parker's office and saw him come hurrying out, clasping a clipboard tightly to his chest. When the girls saw what he was wearing, they clenched their mouths shut in an effort not to burst into laughter. He had on beige safari shorts and a safari jacket. Even his knee socks matched his outfit. On his head he wore a white safari helmet.

"Here comes *dear* Mr. Parker now." Liza giggled.

"I hope he doesn't plan to hunt any big game," Bruce said in a low voice.

Jannette laughed uproariously at his remark.

"I guess she doesn't mind when *he* makes fun of our fearless leader," Chris whispered to Sam.

Sam rolled her eyes but didn't have time to answer. Mr. Parker had come into the middle of the group. His eyes were watery and his nose was red. It was obvious that he was still in the grip of whatever illness had kept him out of work the day before.

He sneezed loudly into a handkerchief. "I'm in no mood for this," he announced, wiping his nose. "So let's all cooperate and get it over with."

By now the group of children milling around had grown to twelve, ranging from ages five to nine.

"Look," whispered Liza, squeezing Chris and Sam on the arm.

Approaching the group were Harrison Springfield and Moira Alezandro, with little Jason between them. Liza was about to greet them, but Jannette stepped in front of her. "Hi there, Jason," she said in her sickly sweet voice. "I'm so happy that you're coming to the zoo today."

"Are we going to see monkeys?" asked Jason eagerly.

"Sure thing," Jannette answered.

The tall, handsome actor ruffled his son's hair. "Take good care of my little guy," he said in a voice that was familiar to all of them from his movies.

"Oh, don't you worry," cooed Jannette, taking Jason's hand. "I promise to keep my eye on him personally. You can count on me. You bet."

"I'm going to throw up," Liza muttered.

When all the children were assembled, Mr. Parker checked them off on a list and then led them out to a van that waited at the front entrance. The children were seated first.

Then Mr. Parker took a moment to talk to his staff. "Don't take your eyes off these kids for one second," he instructed, his red-rimmed eyes watering more by the second. "I want this to be a nice, uneventful day at the zoo. Understand?"

They all nodded. Mr. Parker turned to Chris. "Understand?" he repeated pointedly.

"Yes, sir," she answered in a small voice, embarrassed to be singled out like that in front of Bruce.

"Just to be on the safe side, I want you to stay with Jannette," Mr. Parker told Chris.

"Don't you worry about a thing," said Jannette. "Chrissy will be just fine with me. Won't you, Chrissy?"

Chris wrinkled her nose at Jannette, but threw in a phony grin because she knew Mr. Parker was watching her carefully. "Sure, Jannette, it'll be great."

"I'm going to split you up into two groups," Mr. Parker continued. "Miss Velez, I want you to go with Jannette and Miss Brown."

"Excuse me, Mr. Parker," said Jannette, "but don't you think we should have a man in each group? Maybe Bruce should come with Chrissy and me."

Mr. Parker nodded at Jannette. "Good point. Yes, Bruce, you go with Jannette."

They got into the van and found seats among the kids. Mr. Parker sat behind the gray-haired driver. Bruce sat down behind Jason Springfield. Jannette sweetly told the little girl sitting next to Jason to move so that she could sit next to him — directly in front of Bruce, of course.

"That girl really gets on my nerves," Liza whispered to Chris as she wedged herself into a spot on one of the bench seats in the rear of the van. Chris nodded and watched as Jannette put her arm over Jason's shoulder and then casually turned in her seat to talk to Bruce. Her long, blond hair fell prettily over the back of the seat and her pearly white smile gleamed brightly. Chris felt like a clumsy, ugly clod compared to her. She might as well forget all about Bruce — she was no competition for Jannette.

Jannette let out a shrill peal of laughter at something Bruce said. She sounded so obviously phony to Chris, and she briefly wondered how such an unappealing personality could lurk within such a perfect face and body. She also wondered how she was going to avoid clobbering Jannette if she called her Chrissy in that phony voice one more time. She'd have to, though. Slugging Jannette would definitely be strike three as far as Mr. Parker was concerned.

Chris shifted in her seat and decided she'd be incredibly nice to Jannette today. Because if there were any problems between them, she knew Jannette would tell Mr. Parker, and blame it all on Chris. Everything had to go right today. Chris's job depended on it.

# Chapter Ten

The zoo was almost a half-hour drive from Bonita Beach. Sam kept the kids busy by leading them in songs she'd learned at summer camp the year before. Chris admired her ease with the kids. She had a natural, easygoing way with them.

Liza wasn't shy around kids, either. Caring for her younger twin brothers had obviously given her the confidence to take charge in difficult situations. When the five-year-old girl sitting next to her suddenly panicked at being away from her mother, Liza cheered her up by asking questions about the soft rag doll the girl clutched fearfully in her hands.

Chris wished she had the same assurance, but the truth was, she'd never spent any time around small children. They intimidated her. She didn't know what to say to them, and she was counting on Liza and Sam to take over on this trip. *Oh, well,* she thought, *as annoying as Jannette is, at least she knows how to deal with kids, too.*

The van pulled into the parking lot of the zoo and everyone got out at the front gate. Mr. Parker divided the thirteen children into two groups. He assigned the group of six older children to Chris's group and kept the seven younger ones for his own, which included Liza and Sam. "This way the younger children can move more slowly, at their own pace," he explained.

Chris soon saw that this idea was a sensible one. Though they started out together, the older children quickly got ahead of the younger ones.

There was another reason that Chris's group got ahead of the others: Jannette. She'd naturally assumed the role of group leader and was moving the kids along briskly, never letting them linger too long at any one place.

*Boy, if I were a kid I would hate being rushed like this*, thought Chris, as Jannette hurried them through the bird house. There were separate areas inside the long, narrow house. Behind a mesh net, each section recreated the environment of the birds housed within it. There was a clifflike setting made of huge boulders and covered with scrubby plants for the hawks. Nearby, a darkened compartment had been built for nighttime birds like owls, and hummingbirds whirred in honeysuckle bushes. But the children barely got a chance to see any of them because Jannette kept clapping her hands sharply and moving them along to the next exhibit.

"Jannette, can we go slower?" inquired Arnie, a boy with red hair and freckles.

"Yeah, I want to go back and see the owls again," added Theodore, a dark-haired boy with glasses.

"No, no, no," Jannette replied crisply. "We have to see everything."

"So what if they miss a few exhibits?" Chris asked. "It won't ruin the trip."

Jannette gazed at Chris as if she were trying her patience. "I think I know what I'm doing, Chrissy," she said in an irritated voice. "I'm an experienced baby sitter, you know."

"But these kids don't even know what they're looking at. Slow down," Chris argued. "I think you're going too fast."

"I'm not the one Mr. Parker is worried about, am I?" Jannette retorted. Her expression was so superior that it was all Chris could do to keep from hauling off and hitting her.

Chris looked to Bruce for support, but he was busy showing two twin girls with long blond braids how to call to a red cardinal in a transplanted pine tree. The cardinal answered his call. She wondered how he had learned to do that, since there were no cardinals in Florida.

Their next stop was the monkey habitat. A chain-link fence surrounded a path that threaded through tall trees. Behind the path, different kinds of monkeys swung through the trees. Some of the monkeys were friendly and jabbered at the kids.

Delighted, Jason Springfield called to the monkeys, imitating their high-pitched sounds with remarkable accuracy.

"Come on, keep moving," Jannette ordered the group in her official-sounding voice. The children hurried along the path out of the thicket of trees. Chris noticed Jason cast a reluctant glance over his shoulder as he hesitated and then caught up with the others.

The path led to a series of different moats separating islands on which the gorillas, orangutans, and baboons lived separately. The children clamored around the surrounding fence. At the gorilla exhibit, a pudgy boy in a striped shirt beat his chest and let out an ear-splitting Tarzan yell.

Bruce and Chris laughed, but Jannette was not amused. "Stop that, Ralph!" she snapped. "This is a public place and I expect you to act like a little gentleman."

"I was just fooling around," Ralph complained as Jannette moved them through the exhibit and on to the snake house.

When they reached the snake house, it was feeding time. A man with high leather boots stepped into a cage of boa constrictors. He let several small gray mice loose in the cage.

"Cool," said Theodore.

"Wow!" cried Arnie.

"We're not watching this. It's too disgusting," Jannette told them. "Let's go. I hate snakes."

"I want to see it," Arnie protested.

Cries of "Yeah!" and "Me, too!" rose up from the other children.

"Why don't I stay with anyone who wants to watch and you can go ahead with the others?" Bruce suggested to Jannette.

Jannette didn't seem happy with this idea, but since Bruce had suggested it, she agreed. "Who wants to come with me?" she asked.

No one volunteered. "Come with me, Ursula, Heidi," she told the twins. "I'm sure *you* don't want to see these revolting snakes."

"We love snakes," Ursula informed her. Heidi nodded enthusiastically.

For a moment Jannette looked flustered, then she took charge once again. "Look, I insist. A snake house is no place for children. You'll have nightmares. Come on." With another clap of her hands she led the group out of the snake house.

"Nice try," Chris said to Bruce.

He shrugged his broad shoulders. "I guess Jannette knows what she's doing," he said. "I don't really know how to handle little kids yet."

"I suppose," said Chris doubtfully.

Chris wondered why Jannette was rushing the kids through the zoo. Maybe it was because she was nervous. Chris didn't think so, though. Jannette seemed pretty sure of herself. Chris decided that Jannette was just plain bossy. She'd made up her mind that they were going to see every single exhibit

— and that was that. It didn't matter what the kids wanted. Jannette had a plan and she was going to stick to it. Maybe she thought Mr. Parker would be impressed that they had covered so much ground. Whatever the reason, it was clearly going to be Jannette's way or no way at all.

Chris was distracted from her thoughts by the buzz of whispers among the six children. She saw Arnie and Theodore going from kid to kid, whispering in their ears. She saw Heidi nod at Arnie and then whisper in her sister's ear.

"What's going on?" Chris asked Ursula casually. The girl looked up at Chris with innocent brown eyes and shrugged her narrow shoulders. "Nothing."

"What's all the whispering about?"

"Nothing," Ursula repeated.

They neared the area where the elephants were kept. Chris noticed Arnie and Theodore looking around anxiously. Heidi and Ursula covered their mouths and began to giggle quietly. Ralph and Jason looked very serious, as though they were worried about something.

"Jannette," Chris said, taking the girl's arm to slow her down as she headed at a quick clip toward the elephants. "I think something is going on with these kids."

"What could possibly be going on?" asked Jannette, frowning at Chris.

"I don't know, but something's up. I just sense it."

Jannette chuckled smugly. "Don't let your imagination run away with you, Chrissy. I'm sure there's nothing — "

At that moment, Arnie let out a shrill whistle. "Now!" he shouted.

# Chapter Eleven

"Stop it! Stop it!" Jannette screeched, stamping her foot angrily. "Come back here!"

At Arnie's command, all the children had run off, scattering in different directions. Chris watched, dumbstruck. She knew they were planning some mischief, but she hadn't expected this!

Bruce caught her eye. He looked equally shocked, though there was a glimmer of laughter in his blue eyes. Still wide-eyed with disbelief, Chris felt a wave of uneasy laughter rise up in her throat. This was so awful it was funny!

"This *isn't* funny!" Jannette shrieked at Chris. "What are we going to do?" All her superior calm had disappeared along with the children. Now she was frantic. Her head kept pivoting around and her arms flailed wildly as she spoke. "I can't believe they did that. Those little brats! Those monsters!"

"Okay, calm down," Bruce said to her kindly. "We'll

just have to go round them up."

"We'll never find them," Jannette wailed. "We have to get Mr. Parker." Jannette suddenly looked Chris directly in the eye. "This is your fault, you know."

Chris's jaw dropped. "Mine?"

"Yes. I was in front, leading the group. You were bringing up the rear. You should have seen this coming."

"I told you something was — "

"I can't keep track of everything," she said, cutting Chris off. "I'm not taking the blame for this. I'm telling Mr. Parker you haven't been paying any attention to the kids this whole trip. You've been taking your good old time, looking around at the animals."

"That's what you're *supposed* to do at a zoo, Jannette," Chris argued. "I was helping the kids look at the animals — not that they could even see them with you walking so fast."

"I told you, it's not my fault. And I'm going to find Mr. Parker now and tell him what you did," Jannette said angrily.

A voice sounded in Chris's mind: *Strike three, you're out.* If Jannette convinced Mr. Parker that this was Chris's fault — and it looked like he would believe anything she said — it would be the last straw. Mr. Parker would fire Chris immediately.

That would mean disappointing her parents once again, and having no one to hang out with all summer. It would also mean not being near Bruce. "Don't do that, Jannette," Chris said. "We'll just find the kids and no one will ever know what happened."

"Let's at least give it a try," Bruce suggested.

Jannette shifted from side to side. It was obvious that she didn't want to go along with Chris, but she didn't want to argue with Bruce, either. "All right," she agreed, pouting.

Chris relaxed slightly. She was out of danger for the moment. Now all they had to do was find the children.

Bruce looked at his thick, black-banded watch. "Let's split up and meet back here in a half-hour. That would be at one o'clock."

"Okay," Chris agreed. "Drag back as many kids as you can find and we'll go from there."

Once again, panic took hold of Jannette. "Look at all these people!" she whined, gesturing wildly at the crowd in front of them. "It won't work."

Bruce took Jannette gently by the shoulders and pointed her in the direction of the elephants. "I think Arnie and Ralph went that way," he said. With slumped shoulders, looking defeated already, Jannette headed off.

"You go that way and I guess I'll go this way," Bruce said to Chris. "Good luck."

"Thanks." Chris kept glancing around as she walked along the wide pathways of the zoo. She could see why Jannette was so upset. There were crowds of people in front of every habitat. It was possible that the kids could be standing in the crowds right in front of her and she wouldn't even notice them.

She walked for a while, bending and checking the face of every small person she passed. She passed the lions, tigers and leopards on their large islands. Trying to check places that would attract kids, she went through the farmland exhibit with its cows, goats and pigs. But she didn't have any luck there.

She walked over to the bird exhibit to read the time from a clock that was mounted on a lamppost. It was twelve forty-five, only fifteen minutes before she was supposed to report back to Bruce and Jannette. She hoped they were having better luck than she was. Otherwise, she knew she might as well kiss her job at the Palm good-bye. Chris looked back over her shoulder at the bird house. They'd rushed through it, and maybe some of the kids had wanted to go back and take a better look at an exhibit that had interested them. She was about to go in when the sound of squawking flamingos at the side of the bird house grabbed her attention.

Curious, she walked over to the flamingo area, a grassy hill that came out from the side wall of the bird house. At the bottom of its slope was a marshy river. The area was closed off with only a low gate. A "No Trespassing" sign was all that prevented people from entering the area. Apparently the flamingos liked it there and felt no desire to escape.

Chris instantly saw what the problem was. Heidi and Ursula were chasing the tall, pink birds as a crowd of people watched. Some laughed and seemed to find the sight of the harried birds amusing. Others

98

were outraged and Chris heard remarks like, "Where are their parents?" and "Those poor birds."

Ursula and Heidi took no notice of the crowd. They ran, their blond braids bobbing behind them, with outstretched arms and gleeful giggles. Their matching blue one-piece short sets were smeared with mud, as were their faces and hands. Everywhere they ran, they sent the birds flapping their wide, pink wings and hurrying off in the opposite direction.

They seemed to be having so much fun that for a moment, Chris hated to interfere. She knew she had to, though. She stepped over the fence and made her way down the hill. "Come on, now, Heidi, Ursula!" she called. "It's time to go."

The girls looked up at her and ran into the marshy water. "Come on, girls, you're scaring the birds," Chris coaxed.

"No!" Ursula shouted. "We want flamingos to take home with us."

"You can't take the animals from the zoo home," Chris explained to the little girl. "They're happy here."

"I want a flamingo!" Ursula shouted, while Heidi nodded her head vigorously in agreement.

"You can't have one. Now come on." Chris bent forward to take Ursula's hand. She had it for a second, but Ursula wriggled free, throwing Chris off-balance. Plop! She slipped onto the slippery, muddy ground.

The titter of laughter from above made her acutely

aware of the crowd witnessing this entire scene. Mortified, she stood up and wiped the seat of her now mud-caked shorts. Ursula and Heidi had waded out into the middle of the knee-deep water. Chris didn't want to step into the dark water without her shoes, and she was reluctant to get her sneakers wet. "Ursula, Heidi, please," she begged.

"We want flamingos!" Ursula insisted. Heidi supported her twin's statement by folding her arms over her chest, a determined expression on her face.

Chris was desperate. Any minute now a guard was going to show up and this would change from an embarrassing episode to a major humiliation. Then she had an idea. "We can get some at the gift shop," she told the twins, remembering the fuzzy pink toy flamingos she had seen dangling from cords at the gift shop on her last visit to the zoo.

Ursula and Heidi looked at one another. Heidi nodded. "Okay," said Ursula.

"Hey, you kids, get out of there!" a guard yelled from above.

"We're coming. Sorry!" Chris called back, taking Ursula and Heidi by the hands. They walked through the flock of wary flamingos back up to the top of the hill.

"Can't you read the sign?" the guard scolded Chris when they got to the top of the embankment and stepped over the low fence.

"I had to go down and get them," Chris replied apologetically.

The guard seemed content to leave the incident alone and walked off without another word. Holding the twins' dirty hands firmly, Chris headed back toward the spot where she was supposed to meet up with Bruce and Jannette. "Where did the other kids go?" she asked the girls.

Heidi and Ursula shrugged their shoulders at the same time.

"We all wanted to get away from Jannette," Ursula explained. "She walks too fast. She's crabby, too."

Despite everything, Chris had to smile. It was hard to be angry at the twins. They'd only done what Chris herself would have done in their position — though she wished they had skipped the flamingo-catching mission.

When they neared the meeting place, Chris was relieved to see Bruce sitting on a bench with Ralph and Theodore. She deposited Ursula and Heidi onto the bench beside them.

"What happened?" Bruce asked, staring at her muddy clothing.

"I'll tell you later," Chris answered. "Where's Jannette?"

As if in answer to Chris's question, at that moment they heard Jannette's sharp, angry voice coming up the path behind them. "I've had it with you, you little brat. I'm going to tell your parents what you called me. I swear I am!"

Alarmed, Bruce and Chris ran to meet her. They saw her dragging Arnie up the path, both of her hands wrapped around the boy's upper arm.

"If you don't let go of me, I'm going to punch you," Arnie threatened.

"Go ahead. Try it," Jannette said without a trace of humor.

"Come on, you guys," Bruce said, separating Jannette and the boy. "Break it up."

"I want to see the zoo on my own," Arnie shouted. "That witch is spoiling the whole day."

"Who are you calling a witch, carrot-head!" Jannette countered.

Chris grabbed Jannette's arm. "Cool down. He's just a kid," she said.

Jannette shook her arm free. "He is not. He's a monster!"

Chris couldn't believe her ears. Jannette was losing it, and fast.

Bruce managed to convince Arnie to cooperate. Chris realized that they'd left the other children unattended. She ran back to the bench ahead of the others and was relieved to find them still sitting there dutifully.

Except for some panic and her messed-up shorts, this hadn't been such a disaster, she told herself. They had managed to round up everybody before Mr. Parker found out about the whole mess.

Then she looked again. There was still one child missing. They hadn't found Jason Springfield.

# Chapter Twelve

When Jannette got the news that Jason Springfield was still missing, her face turned a ghastly white, as if she were about to faint.

"Put your head down between your legs," Chris instructed, helping the girl to a bench.

"I can't believe I lost Jason Springfield," Jannette muttered miserably. "It's going to be on the front page of the *Bonita Beach Star*. Forget that, I'll probably see myself on the front of the *National Tattletale*."

"We'll find Jason," Chris said confidently, patting Jannette on the back.

Jannette suddenly jumped up and looked at Chris with the blazing eyes of a lunatic. "I'm not responsible for this, Brown!" she shouted.

Chris wondered how she'd gone from being called Chrissy to being called by her last name.

"If we'd gotten Mr. Parker when I wanted to, we'd have Jason," Jannette insisted. "But now we've lost all this time! Who knows how far he's gotten?" she wailed.

"I don't think he's been able to charter a boat to the Bahamas yet," Chris snapped back. "I'm sure he's still right here at the zoo."

Irritated as she was at Jannette, and as worried as she was about Mr. Parker, a new fear now seized Chris. What if something really had happened to Jason Springfield? What if someone recognized him as Harrison Springfield's son and kidnapped him?

Chris's hands began to tremble at the thought. That poor little boy! *Calm down,* she told herself. *It won't help to panic.* Jannette no longer looked as if she were about to faint. In fact, her face had made a remarkable transition from white to crimson. "I'm going to get Mr. Parker this instant," she said. "And then you'll be sorry."

"You don't even know where he is," Bruce reminded her. "We're not supposed to meet him until two o'clock."

"I'll find him," Jannette assured Bruce as she stormed off.

Bruce and Chris looked at one another. "Where could that kid have run off to?" asked Bruce.

"I don't know," Chris replied. "I hope he's okay."

Bruce nodded. "I suppose we should wait here until Jannette gets back with Mr. Parker. He's going to flip. That guy's a maniac when things are going *well.* This will probably send him over the edge."

Chris winced at his words. She knew he was right.

It wouldn't be so bad if Mr. Parker would just fire her and be done with it. She'd almost accepted that already. But she'd have to listen to all his ranting and raving — and look like an idiot in front of Bruce, too.

"Would you mind staying here alone with the kids?" she asked Bruce. "I'd rather not be here when Mr. Parker shows up. I'm sure Jannette will convince him that this is all my fault."

"She's just upset," Bruce said. "I don't think she'd really blame you. It's no more your fault than it is mine or hers. If you're to blame, then so am I."

"Jannette won't tell Mr. Parker that, though," Chris said glumly.

"Why not?" asked Bruce.

"Because . . . " Chris hesitated. "Because she just won't."

Bruce's mouth curved into a half-smile and he nodded. He seemed to know that what Chris was saying was true. "But Jannette won't try to get you into trouble when it really comes time to talk to Parker," he said. "She's just flipped out right now over this thing. I don't think she'd do that to you."

*Bruce doesn't know Jannette at all,* thought Chris. He was so taken with her that he didn't realize *this* was the real Jannette — spiteful and mean. Chris had seen this side of Jannette in school over the years. But even she had never seen Jannette become so hysterical before.

Chris knew that taking off wasn't the right thing to do. Still, she couldn't convince herself to stick around for the mortifying scene that was bound to occur when Mr. Parker showed up and started screaming at her. What was the point? She already knew he would fire her.

Chris's eyes suddenly filled with tears, which surprised her. She'd thought she had her emotions under control. "I'm sorry, Bruce," she said in a choked voice, fighting to keep the tears from falling. "I have to get out of here, that's all."

Bruce looked at her sympathetically. "I guess I wouldn't want old Parker bellowing at me in front of everyone, either," he admitted.

"Thanks," she said as she ducked her head so he wouldn't see the first tear roll down her cheek. With her head still down, she walked off toward the front entrance of the zoo. She had fifteen dollars in her pocket. If she were lucky, maybe she could find a taxi and have the driver take her home. She'd go as far as fifteen dollars would take her, which would probably be most of the way, and then she'd walk the rest. What other choice did she have? She was certainly not going to sit in that van after Mr. Parker chewed her out in public.

*Typical, Christine,* she scolded herself. *Another chapter in your life ending in utter humiliation. No surprise there.* Chris reached the front gates of the zoo and stopped. A cab pulled up to the parking lot outside the gate and let out a woman and small child. Perfect. She wouldn't even have to go through the trouble of looking up the numbers of cab companies in the phone book. "Wait! Wait!" she called, running through the gate to the taxi.

The driver saw her and she bounded off the curb and over to the driver's open window. In just a few minutes she'd be driving away from the zoo, Mr. Parker, Jannette and Jason Springfield.

Chris thought about the little boy with his big, brown eyes and tousled, sandy blond hair. He'd seemed like a nice kid. She remembered how sweet his room had looked with the pictures of monkeys taped all over it.

That was it! "Monkeys!" she said to the driver as she reached his rolled-down window. "Of course, monkeys!"

The driver looked at her irritably. "Get out of here, you screwy kid," he barked, rolling up his window and taking off.

Chris didn't care. She turned and ran back into the zoo as fast as she could. She didn't stop running until she'd reached the monkey section of the zoo. *Why didn't I think of this before?* They hadn't been able to fit the monkey habitat into Jannette's schedule — they had walked right past it! And monkeys were the animals Jason loved the most.

Breathlessly, she hurried through the koala habitat, then past the gorillas, baboons and orangutans until she reached the monkey section. Chris scanned the area. There was no sign of Jason. Her shoulders slumped in disappointment. She'd been so sure!

Then she spotted him. He was sitting on the

ground, quietly feeding peanuts from a bag to a small monkey. The look on his face said it all: He was incredibly happy. Chris couldn't bear to interrupt him right away. She hung back and watched the little monkey reach through the chain-link fence and take the nuts which Jason offered from his flat palm.

Knowing that he wasn't really supposed to be feeding the animals, however, Chris decided to approach him after a few minutes had gone by.

"Hi," she said, sitting down beside him. At her approach, the little monkey scampered off into the trees. Jason frowned, but after a minute or so he seemed to accept the monkey's disappearance. "We've been looking for you," said Chris.

Jason grimaced. "Am I in trouble?" he asked.

"You shouldn't have run away," Chris told him.

"The other kids were doing it, and I wanted to see the monkeys," Jason said. "I know it was bad."

Chris smiled. "If it makes you feel any better, I'm in trouble, too, for letting you guys run away."

"Oops," said Jason, covering his mouth. "I didn't think big people got in trouble."

"I'm not exactly big people yet," Chris told him with a laugh. "I'm kind of a medium-sized person. Like the sodas at the movies — small, medium and large."

Jason giggled. "Do we have to go back?" he asked.

"Yep," said Chris, getting up.

He continued to sit. "Let's stay here. That way we won't get into trouble."

"If we stay, you won't see your mom and dad

again," Chris said.

He thought about that for a moment and then rose to his feet.

Chris took his hand and waved to the monkeys with her free hand. "So long, guys," she said.

"So long, guys," Jason repeated, waving.

They walked back to the spot near the elephants where Chris had left Bruce. She stopped several yards away when she saw Mr. Parker giving orders to three zoo guards. He was very upset, and pointing frantically in all directions. Sam and Liza stood beside him, watching over the little children in their charge. They both looked worried to death. Bruce was still watching the five older children, and Jannette stood beside Mr. Parker, her face puffy and red from crying.

*Who can that be?* Chris wondered, noticing a man she didn't recognize in the group. He held a pad and pencil in his hand, and he was going from person to person, writing down notes as he spoke to them. Around his neck was draped a fairly large, boxy camera with a long lens.

Sam was the first to spot Chris. She smiled and waved wildly. "There's Chris — and she's got Jason!" she shouted. "I told you she wouldn't just leave," she said loudly to Mr. Parker.

Mr. Parker stopped talking to the guards and looked at Chris and Jason as they joined the group. "Thank heavens!" he exclaimed dramatically. "We're not going to be sued for billions, after all."

Mr. Parker took Jason's hand from Chris and led him over to Bruce. "Now stay there and don't move," he instructed the small boy, who seemed confused. Then he went back to the guards and assured them that everything was all right. He thanked them for their help with a haughty sniff, as though he were dismissing servants.

In the meantime, Chris joined Liza and Sam. "Where did you find him?" asked Liza.

"With the monkeys. All of a sudden, I remembered how crazy he was about them."

"That was using your head," Sam said proudly. "Mr. Parker should be impressed by that."

"You mean Jannette didn't tell him that I was responsible for this whole mess?"

Liza cleared her throat uncomfortably. "I did hear her say something along those lines, I'm afraid."

"I knew it," said Chris. "What did Bruce tell him?"

"He acted kind of dumb and said he didn't know. Maybe you left, maybe you were looking for Jason. He wasn't sure," Liza told her. "You weren't really going to leave, were you?"

"I told Bruce I was going to, but I couldn't do it," Chris explained.

"We told Mr. Parker you wouldn't," said Sam, putting her arm around Chris's shoulder.

Chris looked toward Mr. Parker and saw that he was trying to get rid of the man with the pad of paper who seemed insistent on talking to him. "Who is that guy?" she asked Liza and Sam.

"He's a reporter for the *Bonita Beach Star*," said Sam. "He just happened to be at the zoo when he heard from one of the guards that Jason Springfield was missing. He ditched his wife and kids and has been hanging around here ever since, trying to get a story."

Chris looked again and saw that the man had persuaded Mr. Parker to speak, after all. Curious to hear what he was saying, she moved closer to him.

"The staff at the Palm Pavilion Hotel is usually completely reliable," Mr. Parker was telling the man, who was rapidly writing down all of the information. "These things happen and . . . to tell you the truth, I'm not exactly clear on the exact chain of events. Perhaps Jannette could help you on that."

The reporter turned to Jannette, who immediately seized the spotlight. "I don't really know how this happened," she said with a wave of her hand. "I was watching the kids very carefully every second. I personally promised Harrison Springfield I would look after his son today, and I did. But then — " Jannette caught sight of Chris standing behind the reporter. "Well, it was all her fault, really," she said, pointing at Chris.

The reporter turned around and brought his camera up to his face. With a quick click he snapped a picture, capturing Chris's startled expression.

Chris stepped back, speechless. She could see it now — her picture on the front page underneath a headline reading: ALL HER FAULT!

# Chapter Thirteen

"That's not exactly true." Bruce stepped forward. "I don't really think it was anybody's fault. The kids just got away from us. They thought they were being funny. They were just being kids, I guess."

"I didn't mean it was *your* fault, Bruce," said Jannette. "Not at all. But Chris should have — "

"Miss Brown, I have warned you," Mr. Parker began, a menacing look on his face. "Why is it that every time you are involved in a project there is some sort of foul-up?"

Chris braced herself. The moment she had been dreading was about to come.

"If anything had happened to Jason Springfield—"

"Chris is the one who found Jason," Bruce reminded Mr. Parker.

Mr. Parker sighed. "Yes, but why did these children run off in the first place?"

"We were escaping *her*!" Arnie cried, pointing at

Jannette. "She was ruining the whole trip."

Jannette giggled nervously. "That's a funny little joke, Arnie," she said between clenched teeth.

"I'd say Chris saved the day. Wouldn't you, Jannette?" Bruce said, gallantly deflecting the attention away from Arnie's charges.

Jannette stuck her lip out in a sulky pout. "Well, I suppose — "

"That's right!" said the reporter, coming up close to Chris. "You were the one who returned with the Springfield kid. How did you find him? Did you feel he was in any danger? What did you say to get him to return with you?"

Chris didn't know what to say. She was so overwhelmed — and overjoyed — that Bruce had come to her aid like that. Her heart was pounding in her chest. So much was happening so fast. She simply stared at the reporter, speechless.

"I'm a good friend of Chris Brown's and I've always known her to think fast on her feet," Liza said, stepping up to the reporter and making sure he noticed her.

"Can I quote you on that?" asked the reporter.

"Oh, absolutely. My name is Liza Velez. Chris and I have been friends since we were little. She's always been brave. I remember a time back in third grade when the class bully . . . "

Liza's voice seemed to drift away as Chris looked past the reporter, Mr. Parker and Jannette. She smiled at Bruce. He smiled back, then gave her the thumbs-up signal, just as he had the other day when she had jumped into the pool. Only this time there was nothing teasing about it. It was a genuine thumbs-up.

"Why not get a picture of Chris with Jason?" Sam suggested, putting her arm around the boy and guiding him in front of Chris.

"Great idea," said the reporter. He lifted his camera and took a few shots of Chris and Jason.

"How about one with me and my two best friends?" said Chris, knowing how much Liza would enjoy being in the newspaper. She put her arms around Sam and Liza and the reporter took their picture.

"That's quite enough," said Mr. Parker, blowing his nose into a white handkerchief. "My twelve-hour cold tablet is running out and the van driver is waiting for us. I suggest we get going."

They followed Mr. Parker's lead as he walked at his usual brisk clip toward the front gate. Chris hung back from the group a little. She wanted to talk to Bruce. "Thanks a lot," she told him as he came up beside her.

"Hey, it wasn't fair for you to take the blame," he replied. "I just told the truth."

Chris glanced at Jannette, who was walking by with her chin up in the air. "I think Jannette is mad at us," she said.

Bruce shrugged. "She'll get over it."

"I guess she will," Chris agreed, smiling.

The trip home was a quiet one. Even the children

seemed exhausted from all the excitement of the day. By the time the van left them off at the hotel, Chris was so tired that the bike ride home felt like nothing short of torture.

That night, Chris soaked in a bubble bath. Her leg muscles and feet hurt. She had a stripe of sunburn across her nose and a blister on the back of her heel from walking around all day in her new white sneakers.

But she was happy. Blissfully happy. *I'd say Chris saved the day. Wouldn't you, Jannette?* She played Bruce's words over and over in her head. It was too unbelievable!

After her bath, Chris wrapped herself in her white terry robe. On her way to her room, she passed by her parents, who were sitting in the living room. Her mother was correcting papers and her father was reading the newspaper. Her mother looked up and smiled.

"Getting ready for bed?" she asked, taking off her glasses.

"Yep," Chris answered.

"Sweet dreams," said her father, glancing up from his paper.

"Sleep tight," her mother said.

Chris hovered in the doorway for a minute as her parents went back to what they had been doing. She turned toward her bedroom, and then turned back. "All right!" she finally exploded. "What's going on?"

"What do you mean?" Mrs. Brown asked.

"You two always want to know each little detail of everything I do. How come you're not asking me about work? Last night Dad didn't ask, even though I was ironing — something I don't usually do. And now you're not asking again tonight."

Her parents looked at one another and laughed. "Well, you complained that I was always bugging you. Your father and I talked about it and decided maybe we had both been pressuring you," her mother explained.

"Oh," said Chris. It was true. She *had* complained. "Well, today I want you to ask," she said.

"How was work today, Chris?" asked her father.

"Wonderful. Great. The best. I found a kid who had wandered away and gotten lost. And you'll never believe who it was — Harrison Springfield's son!"

"You mean, the actor?" Mrs. Brown looked extremely impressed. She had actually gone to some of Harrison Springfield's movies with Chris, and once she had confessed that she had a little crush on him, too.

Chris nodded. She told her parents the whole story about the trip to the zoo, and about how the reporter had taken her picture. "We're so proud of you," said her mother when Chris finished the story.

"Though I'm not surprised in the least," added her father. "You've always been bright and resourceful."

It was funny. This was the kind of conversation that always drove Chris crazy. But now it sounded great. Maybe because she finally thought that her parents could have been right all along. Maybe she had all the good qualities they thought she had, after all. "Thanks, Dad," she said.

"Don't thank me, it's simply the truth," he replied. "That Harrison Springfield may be a big star, but he should consider himself lucky to have you baby-sit for his kid."

Chris laughed. "Dad, come on."

"It's true," he insisted.

"Well, maybe you're right," she said modestly. "No one else could find Jason but me."

"Exactly," said her mother.

"Good night," Chris said, kissing them both on their cheeks. It suddenly didn't seem so bad to have parents who were interested in her, and who thought she was the greatest.

The next day, Sunday, Chris, Liza and Sam weren't scheduled to work. They spent a few hours together at the beach, hashing over their adventure at the zoo.

"You didn't have it bad at all compared to us," Liza told Chris as she slathered her skin with number eight suntan lotion. "Mr. Parker kept sneezing and blowing his nose. He almost drove the poor little kids nuts, telling them not to get too close to the animals, and not to do this and that. What a pain that guy is!"

Sam covered her nose with yellow zinc oxide. "I think Bruce likes you," she said to Chris. "He must, the way he stuck up for you and all."

"I don't know," Chris replied, pulling the brim of

**117**

her red sun visor down lower over her face. She'd already gotten too much sun on her fair skin in the last week. "Maybe he's just a nice guy. I know he doesn't *dis*like me, but I don't think he *likes* me, likes me. He might still be stuck on Jannette."

"After he saw what a jerk she is?" cried Liza.

Chris rolled onto her stomach. "It's hard to tell. You know guys. They're tough to figure out."

"That's the truth," Liza agreed.

Sam got to her feet and ran a few paces toward the water. "Last one in will marry Mr. Parker someday!" she called back to them. In an instant, Liza and Chris were on their feet, racing her into the water.


On Monday, the girls reported to work and punched their timecards in the kitchen. "Get a load of this!" cried Sam, laughing. She'd been reading the work schedule tacked onto the wall and then her eye had wandered over to the day's specials on the menu. The dessert special was called "Chris Brown Betty."

Chris and Liza looked at it with shocked expressions. A low rumbling chuckle behind them made the girls turn around. Chef Alleyne stood watching them, his arms folded across his massive chest, his eyes crinkled with laughter.

"What is a Chris Brown Betty?" Sam asked.

"It's really apple brown betty, but I've added some orange liqueur into the whipped cream. I had to do something to celebrate our heroine," the chef explained.

Chris's hand went to her chest in surprise. "You mean you heard about what happened?"

Chef Alleyne turned back to the pot of soup he was busy seasoning. "Everyone has heard about it. Go ask Mrs. Chan for a copy of the *Bonita Beach Star*. She showed me her copy this morning."

The girls hurried toward the kitchen door. "Thank you for the dessert!" Chris called back to Chef Alleyne. The large man nodded and chuckled once again.

Out at the front desk, they didn't have to ask Mrs. Chan for her paper. Lillian and Sunny were standing together, reading it. "Boy, did we miss all the action!" Sunny joked. "Way to go, Chris."

"Can I see?" Chris asked.

Lillian handed her the paper with a smile. The article was on page six. Above the picture of Chris and Jason read the headline, "Baby Sitter Saves Celeb's Son."

Liza grabbed the paper from Chris and read it out loud in a dramatic voice. " 'On Saturday, the son of superstar Harrison Springfield was rescued by Christine Brown, a staff baby sitter at the posh Palm Pavilion Hotel, during an outing at the Downstate Zoo. Young Jason Springfield mutinied along with five other children when the baby sitter they were assigned to refused to slow down. A full-scale search was conducted by Mr. Oliver C. Parker, the hotel's manager. As twilight descended over the zoo, this reporter could feel the tension in the air as the search continued with no result.'"

"Twilight?" Sam asked. "It wasn't even three in the afternoon."

"This whole article is just a little overblown," Chris had to admit.

Liza read on. "'If it hadn't been for the clever, deductive reasoning of Miss Brown, the star's son might have spent a terrifying night alone in the zoo. Fortunately, the fast-thinking strawberry blonde remembered Jason Springfield's fondness for monkeys and returned to the monkey area — an area cruelly overlooked by the fast-walking baby sitter in charge of young Jason's group.'"

"Jannette is going to have a fit when she reads this," said Sam, laughing.

The article went on to say how Chris had managed to persuade Jason to come to her by brilliantly employing methods of child psychology.

"It looks like you're the local heroine!" Lillian grinned.

"Nah, this guy really exaggerates," said Chris, shrugging. But secretly, she was glad the reporter had written such a big story. She was enjoying being in the spotlight — for the right reason — for once.

At that moment, Harrison Springfield turned the corner of the counter. He was dressed in a crinkly, beige cotton suit. His week in Florida had given him a golden tan that made him more gorgeous than ever.

When he saw Chris, his eyes lit up with recognition. He walked up to her and extended his hand.

"You look more lovely than in your picture," he said, clasping her hand. "I can't thank you enough, Christine."

Chris was dumbstruck. She gazed up at the handsome actor with wide eyes until she managed to find her voice. "Uh, it was my pleasure," she said dreamily.

A low cough caught Chris's attention. She looked and saw Liza and Sam staring at her. They waved shyly. "Those are my best friends. They're big fans of yours, and so am I," Chris told him.

Harrison Springfield beckoned for them to come over with a wave of his hand. Liza's knees buckled slightly as she held onto Sam's arm. "Could I have an autograph?" Liza asked in a small voice.

The actor searched his pocket and came up with a gold pen. He signed his name and wrote a small note on the back of two pieces of hotel stationery that were laid out on the desk.

"I have an idea," he said, looking at Chris. "Give me your copy of the *Bonita Beach Star*. May I?" he asked politely, his pen poised above the article.

"Sure!" said Chris.

He wrote an inscription and then handed the paper to Chris. It said, "To Chris, a true-life heroine. I owe you one — a big one. Thanks from the bottom of my heart. Harrison Springfield."

Chris pressed the paper to her chest. "I'll treasure this forever," she told the actor.

Mr. Parker suddenly emerged from his office.

When he approached the group, Harrison Springfield put his arm around Chris and squeezed her hard. "Mr. Parker, you have a fine girl here," he said. "A real gem. Be sure to hang onto her."

Mr. Parker sniffed and gave Chris a tight smile. "Yes, by all means. She is a diamond in the rough, no doubt."

"Does that mean Chris is off probation?" Sam asked boldly.

Mr. Parker harrumphed and stretched his neck uncomfortably. "I don't suppose it would be very good press to fire a local heroine, now, would it?"

"I think that means yes," said Liza happily.

Mr. Parker nodded curtly and strode off in the direction of the kitchen.

Harrison Springfield was checking out of the hotel that morning. He kissed Chris on the cheek and then went over to settle his account with Mrs. Chan.

Chris ran the tips of her fingers along the newspaper the famous actor had signed. She couldn't wait until her parents saw it! They'd probably frame it. She wouldn't mind, though. She could almost imagine the pride on their faces, and it made her smile.

Liza put her hand on Chris's shoulder as they watched Harrison Springfield walk away. "I love this job," Liza said, sighing.

"So do I," Sam agreed.

Chris just stood there grinning. It was going to be a wonderful summer.

There's a new girl working at the Palm Pavilion. Trisha Royce is blond, beautiful, athletic and rich — and it looks like she's about to become Sam's best friend. Will Chris and Liza lose *their* best friend?

Watch for SITTING PRETTY #2: *True Blue*

## SUZANNE WEYN

Suzanne Weyn is the author of many books for children and young adults. Among them are: *The Makeover Club, Makeover Summer* and the series NO WAY BALLET. Suzanne began baby-sitting at the age of thirteen. Later, while attending Harpur College, she worked as a waitress in a hotel restaurant. Suzanne grew up on Long Island, N.Y., and loves the beach. Sailing, snorkeling, waterskiing and swimming are some of her favorite activities. In SITTING PRETTY she is able to draw on these experiences.

Suzanne now has a baby of her own named Diana, who has two terrific baby sitters — Chris and Joy-Ann.